PYTHON DANCE

Norman Silver

PYTHON·DANCE

DUTTON CHILDREN'S BOOKS   *New York*

Library of Congress Cataloging-in-Publication Data
Silver, Norman. Python dance / by Norman Silver.—1st American ed. p. cm.
Summary: As the fights with her stepfather increase, Ruth, a Jewish South African
teenager, spends more time at her boyfriend's house, trying to hide her less-than-
womanly figure and becoming more aware of her country's oppressive system of
apartheid.   ISBN 0-525-45161-7   [1. Self-acceptance—Fiction. 2. Family
problems—Fiction. 3. Stepfathers—Fiction. 4. South Africa—Race relations—
Fiction. 5. Jews—South Africa—Fiction.] I. Title.   PZ7.S585736Py 1993
[Fic]—dc20   92-47581   CIP AC

First published in the United States 1993
by Dutton Children's Books,
a division of Penguin Books USA Inc.
375 Hudson Street, New York, New York 10014
Originally published in Great Britain 1992
by Faber and Faber Limited, London
Designed by Adrian Leichter
Printed in U.S.A.
First American Edition

10 9 8 7 6 5 4 3 2 1

FEB 13 2009

Young adult
FICTION

176964

PYTHON DANCE

PART ONE

1

I NEVER MY WHOLE LIFE BELIEVED IN THE power of *muti* magic. As a matter of fact, it meant nothing to me. I knew the servants bought *muti* potions from herbalists and witch doctors, but why would a nice Joburg girl want to go messing with a whole load of stuff she didn't even believe in?

All I knew about witch doctors was what I read in my mom's book of South African tribes. And even then I never read the whole book; I just looked at the colorful pictures and read a bit here and there.

For example, there was this recipe for a *muti* medicine that I really liked the sound of. (By the way, you won't find this recipe in the *Goodwill Cookbook.*) Here are the main ingredients:

the fat of a lightning bird
the flesh of a tortoise
the crushed stem of the thunder tree
the feathers of a peacock
the bulb of the Ifafa lily
the fat of a python
the skin of an otter
the sound of thunder
and a flash of lightning.

You might have difficulty in getting some of these ingredients from Fatti and Moni's Foodshop, but if you can get hold of them, use a pounding stick to blend them well in a mixing bowl. This *muti* will protect you from violent storms, so the book said. It was a good *muti*.

But there were also *muti* medicines that could be used to harm other people, the book said, though obviously it didn't want to give recipes for those.

I found out about such things in my own, sad way.

2

The day of the tree-cutting Mom cried from morning to night. She was very superstitious, my mom, and believed that if a tree got deliberately cut down, then someone in that family would die.

She cried like hell, and the more I tried to tell her it was just superstition, the more she cried.

She was an educated woman, Mom was; she had a B.A.

in history and worked for Zlotkin & Hillowitz, the lawyers, so she wasn't stupid or anything. She was just a highly strung person. If a violin was strung as tight as her, it would have folded in half.

"You don't believe anything, Ruthie," she sobbed.

I hated it when Mom called me Ruthie. Ruth was bad enough, but Ruthie was the worst.

"Just you wait, you'll see. When Uncle Joey had the big gum tree chopped down, old Archie had his heart attack, and when Mrs. Weitzman at school had her oak chopped down, she lost her husband in a road accident, and . . ."

"Come on, Mom, you're really morbid."

Her crying was beginning to annoy me, to tell the truth. It was highly embarrassing for one thing, because there must have been about fifty spectators for the big event. All the nannies from up and down our road were sitting on the pavements watching the preparations. And all the garden boys were there too, laughing and jawling with the nannies. And Emily, our servant girl, and John, the garden boy, also watched from the side gate.

"For God's sake, Mom, why are you having the tree cut down, then? Just tell them to stop and that's the end of it."

"We can't. If we don't, the council will sue us."

"Yes, Mom, I know all that."

She had told me about five hundred thousand times that the roots were damaging Noreen Avenue, but no way could I see any damage. The road outside our house looked as flat as the rest of the road.

As we stood there, my sister Lenore came out of the front door of the house, eating a naartjie. She was just two years younger than me, but looking at her eating that fruit, you could have told how completely different she was from me in every way.

Her style of eating a naartjie was to peel it, segment it, then lay all the skyfies in a circle on a plate. Then she used a knife to pip each skyfie. It was all so neat: the peels, the segments, the pips in a pile.

Me? I just peel it then break off chunks with my teeth. I can't taste the blooming thing unless my mouth is filled with a good-sized chunk, at least two or three skyfies.

Lenore ate the skyfies one at a time, delicately. She was so damn pretty, and she knew it. Pretty hands and shapely legs, beautifully combed light-brown hair, pretty face and a well-developed figure for a fourteen-year-old. You would hardly guess we came from the same parents, with my skinny body and skinny legs, until you worked out that she got my mom's looks, and I got my dad's.

As she approached and saw Mom crying, Lenore gave me this piercing look. She always did it—she couldn't even help it anymore—and it meant: why are you tormenting Mom?

She slipped her arm around Mom's waist and hung there like an angel. Mom even managed to give her a smile.

The white man in charge of the operation finished his measuring, and he called one of his African workers over. "OK, Moses, you cut here when we're ready."

Moses picked up the electric saw, walked over to the tree, and switched on his machine.

Someone screamed, and all the nannies and the garden boys jumped up from the pavement to see the action.

"Haaaaaiiiiiii!"

"Switch the blerrie thing off!" the white man yelled. "We're not ready yet."

A black man was scuttling down the tree as fast as lightning.

"Haaaiiii! Don't cut yet!" he shouted. "I'm still in the tree."

Moses was giggling to himself. "I didn't start it yet. I was just checking the electricity."

"Don't arse around here, Moses!" the white man said, wagging his finger.

The man in the tree reached the ground. He had attached two thick ropes to some sturdy branches about thirty feet up. He and a third black man each took hold of these ropes to guide the tree, when it fell, between the house and the garden wall.

A black limousine with darkened windows drew up outside the house. It was the Chinaman doing his afternoon fah-fee round. It was payout time, but when the Chinaman saw so many white people around, he drove past and stopped a few blocks further down the street.

3

All the servants in the area used to play fah-fee with the Chinaman—they called him Chong. They used to bet money on a number, and if that number came up, then they won twenty-four times the amount they put on, but mostly they just lost day after day, and it wasn't surprising because there were thirty-six numbers to bet on. That's why Chong was so rich. I would never have bet with him. It was strictly for losers, that game, but both Emily and John played twice every day without fail. It all revolved around dreams.

"Rootie, what you dream last night?" Emily asked me every so often at breakfast.

Usually I remembered a dream to tell her. For example, just recently, before the tree-cutting, I had dreamt of my auntie who lived in Klerksdorp.

"I was in her swimming pool on the li-lo."

"Is that by your Auntie Bertha?"

"Yes, Bertha P-chinsky."

It was a joke between Mom and me to say the "P" of "Puchinsky" with a disgusting, explosive sound, because neither of us was fond of Harry P-chinsky.

"My hands were hanging over the sides into the water. Then something touched my hands. I looked over the side of the li-lo. It was a fish. Then I noticed lots of fish swimming underneath me. I was scared of them. I sat on top of the li-lo, trying to keep out of the water. But the fish kept bumping my li-lo, and it was difficult to keep my balance. I called to Aunt Bertha for help, but the phone started ringing and she went to answer it."

"Ag, thanks Rootie. I must put ten cents on number thirteen, Big Fish."

Each number had a name like Human Dung, Big Knife, Newborn Baby, Diamond Lady, and your dreams told you which number to bet on. I think it's to do with your ancestors speaking to you in dreams, but why then did Emily use my dreams and not her own? Maybe she believed the dreams of white people had more value—I wouldn't be surprised.

She always placed her bets via a runner. Chong only dealt with the runners who collected money for him in each area. They got a percentage of his profits, plus everyone suspected they pocketed a certain amount before handing their money over to Chong.

4

Mom's crying was tragic. Mannie sat on a deck chair on the veranda reading the newspaper, completely undisturbed by the kerfuffle. Doubtless, he was checking share prices or horse form. Those were the only things I ever saw him do, so if he wasn't reading share prices, you can bet your life he was studying the horses.

Mannie was my stepfather, if you want to know. This bloke with the slick greying hair greased back and a paunch like the belly of an old horse, wearing maroon pajamas with matching slippers in the middle of the afternoon, was actually my mother's husband. I would have died of shame on the spot if that was my husband—or my father, for that matter.

He did have three grown-up kids somewhere, but two of them never came to visit him. I don't blame them one bit. The third one, Milly, kept in touch with him, but everyone knew she was only shloeping him up to get money out of him. I don't know why she bothered—it was like trying to squeeze blood out of a stone.

Of course Mom's crying had no effect on Mannie. He was much more worried about Anglo's price going down three cents than about Mom's blood pressure building up to boiling point. But Mannie couldn't care less. He had watched her cry for eight years and hardly ever put his arm round her to comfort her or anything.

"OK, Moses, let her rip!"

Mom leaned against the veranda wall and sobbed into her arms.

The electric saw started up and began biting its way through the massive trunk. The white man sat on the garden wall directing the operations with his hand, as if he were the conductor of an orchestra.

The nannies kept shouting out things in their own language and laughing at the boys who were cutting the tree.

When the saw had long passed the halfway point, the tree began to show a bit of movement.

"You pull now, Simon!" the white bloke shouted. He was either dead stupid or he had a lot of faith in his skills as an organizer of tree-cutting, because he didn't move the whole time. He just sat under the tree on the garden wall, obviously convinced that it would be guided into the gap between himself and the house.

"Zack! You stchoopid idiot! Pull! Pull, man! It's not a kite you flying. Give it a pull!"

"I'm doing it, baas!"

Zack dug his heels into Mom's neat lawn and pulled.

There was a kind of creaking noise, and the tree bent over at an angle. It was an acacialata, whatever that was. Mom always called it the acacialata. It was huge, with a vast umbrella of branches with broad, fernlike leaves, and I wasn't convinced that it could fit in the gap. But I reckoned these contractors knew what they were doing.

"Slowly, now, Moses! Slow down, man!"

The tree bent over like it was bowing to the audience. Some nannies danced around excitedly on the pavement. Afternoons on Noreen Avenue were usually quite boring. The tree hovered over the lawn. The two boys pulled on their ropes.

Suddenly there was this noise like a shotgun as the trunk split and the tree veered over toward the wall. The white bloke leaped off like a jumping jack, but some of the smaller branches still caught him quite badly.

His three boys just stood and stared. They didn't try to help him or anything. They thought he'd murder them for allowing such a thing to happen.

He was a bit hurt by the branches, mostly scratches on his face, but he didn't make much of it, probably because there was such a big audience.

Then I noticed the garden wall. It was smashed where the huge branches had made contact.

"OK, Mrs. Hirsch, the job's nearly done. My boys will cut it into pieces and take them away tomorrow in the truck. OK?"

Mom looked at the man through her tears. His face was bleeding in a few places, but Mom couldn't have cared less.

"What about the wall?" she said.

"What about it?"

"It's broken," Mom said.

"Ja, it is," the man said.

"So you better fix it," Mom said.

"That's not part of my job, missus. You just asked me to cut a tree."

"Listen, Mr. Pietersen. You damaged my wall and you're going to repair it."

"No way, missus. I didn't damage it. It was an act of God."

"Rubbish!" Mom said.

When Mom got angry, the boot was on the other foot. Even men began to quake behind their beards when she got like that. I think it's because she lived on her own for so long, from the time my real dad died until she remarried the Mannie bloke when I was eight. So that was four years where she had to fend for herself, not counting the years since then, when she's still had to fend for herself.

"If you refuse to repair the damage, you can speak to my lawyer. He'll explain to you the difference between an act of God and bad calculation."

"It wasn't bad calculation, missus. It's because the tree was old. Nobody could have known that it was going to split."

"I'll phone my lawyer, Mr. Pietersen. You just wait a moment."

"No, missus. I'll tell you what. Zack is a bricklayer. He can fix it for you tomorrow."

"Is he any good?"

"I'm telling you, he used to be a brickie before he came to work for me. He'll do a good job. Good as new."

"OK. But it better be good."

The man drove off in his truck. The crowds dispersed. Our garden looked very bare, I thought. That tree used to be a whole world of activity. Pigeons and doves used to fly in and out of it all day, or sit up there in the high branches cooing softly to themselves. That tree also used to be great for climbing. My sister Lenore and my best friend Merle and I used to spend happy-happy hours up there when we were younger. Now the tree was lying there like a giant corpse with all its private nooks and secret branches exposed to the world, and me and Merle weren't young anymore, and Lenore had her own friends.

Mom burst out sobbing again. "Emily, make me some tea please," she said to our servant girl.

"Yes, Madam."

Mannie went inside, probably to phone his stockbroker. He didn't care an inch of spaghetti about the tree or the garden wall. After all, it wasn't his house. Mom and he kept all their finances strictly apart. He paid her a monthly allowance for living in her house, which contributed only a pittance toward his share of the expenses. In my books he wasn't exactly Mr. Generosity—he was an all-time bastard.

5

After the tree-cutting my mom was in a terrible state. And I was pretty depressed myself by the time Alan Gerber phoned me.

"Listen, Alan, you can't phone me every day."

"Why not?"

"Because my stepfather needs the phone for his work. He keeps complaining that it's always engaged."

"Oh. Why don't you just go steady with me? Then I won't need to phone you so often."

"Because I don't want to go steady with anyone, yet."

Alan Gerber, I must tell you, was involved in the mix-up that happened in the first few seconds of the New Year. This is what happened.

I didn't go with Alan to that New Year's party. You see, I met this chap from Grahamstown the summer before. I met him on the beach at Plettenberg Bay where we were on holiday. We played beach tennis and went out a few times, and I think it must have been the holiday air or something, because I got very keen on him, seeing as how good-looking he was, and started corresponding with him once I got back to Joburg. His name was Erroll Pinkus and his hobbies were dancing, debating, and records.

Then, in one letter he tells me he's on his way to Joburg to see me. I was quite overjoyed with the idea until he collected me from the front door. He didn't look anything like I remembered him. I couldn't work it out. Maybe it was the altitude, because Joburg is six thousand feet above sea level, and he looked like he must have gone through a change of appearance every hundred feet or so. And unfortunately the change was in the direction of a sheep. He had this bleating voice, and a sheepish smile, and on top of it all, he wasn't as intelligent as I first thought. (I only used to go out with intelligent boys. That's the first thing I would ask them: "What did you get in your matric?") Not only did he remind me of a sheep, but even worse, a sheep in love. On the way to the party in his uncle's car he told me how he'd been looking forward the whole year to seeing me again.

From the first moment, I wanted to tell him to pack his bags and go back to his flock in Grahamstown, but it wouldn't have been polite just there and then, would it? So I strung along, and he practiced his hobbies with me. The whole night he debated whether Elvis was better than the Beatles. The only trouble was that he debated both points of view and didn't let me get a word in edgeways.

Actually, he was quite good at the cha-cha, and he taught me a few fancy steps. But I wouldn't let him get near me, if you know what I mean. I made him keep his distance, especially as I got very bored with his debating voice.

Anyway, midnight came along, and you could hear the Africans gonging the lampposts and shouting "Heppy! Heppy New Year! Heppy 1967! Heppeeeeeee!" And this Erroll was lurking near me, waiting to give me his New Year kiss. But I couldn't face it, to tell the truth.

Now, all night I was aware that Alan Gerber was watching me. He was with his own girl, of course, but they didn't seem to be hitting it off. I met Alan about six weeks before that party. He was OK—bright and all—but a bit quiet. And you know what they say: still waters run deep. He'd asked me out quite a few times during those six weeks, but I had declined. Yet we had met on two occasions at Balfour Park swimming pool, and I had the feeling neither occasion was accidental. Both times he was nice to me, but boy, was he intense. I had my suspicions that he was too keen on me, and if there's one thing I couldn't stand, it was anyone who was too keen on someone.

Anyway, at this New Year's party I could see Alan out of the corner of my eye, and he was avoiding his girlfriend like mad. And I was avoiding this Erroll Pinkus like mad. And so, of course, we bumped into each other under this trellis that had a vine growing on it.

We smiled at each other, and what with the excitement of all the Africans gonging the lampposts and all that, Alan suddenly hugged me and gave me this really meaningful Happy New Year kiss. Jeez, what was I letting myself in for?

Although he wasn't good-looking in a film-star sort of

way, his face had a lot of character. At least he didn't remind a person of a certain woolly creature. He had these brown eyes that asked a million questions per second—very gentle, but boy, did they search you out sometimes.

He obviously thought I was giving him the go-ahead to marry me there and then, and I had to say to him, "Hold on, man! It's only a New Year's kiss."

"Only a New Year's kiss!" he said. "How do you kiss the rest of the year?" And he tried to hug me some more.

But at that moment Erroll Pinkus turns up.

"There you are," he said to me, showing off his remarkable powers of perception. "What are you doing with this guy?"

"Well, it's none of your business actually," Alan said, "but if you must know, we're checking out these grapevines."

"Don't mess with me, man!" Erroll said, looking as mean as a merino.

"I've known this guy a long time, Erroll," I said, trying to calm things down, "and he's . . ."

"He's your boyfriend, is he?" Erroll asked.

"Ja, do you want to make something of it?" Alan said, his eyes searching into Erroll's.

Before something nasty developed, up came this blond girl with red lips that looked like they came out of a Lucky packet, and she said, "Alan, come dance, or are you deserting me?"

Alan looked at me, and I shrugged my shoulders. I turned to Erroll.

"Come on, take me home. I want to go."

The blond popsy hauled Alan toward the music. He

looked back over his shoulder and pretended to dial a telephone. That meant he'd phone me.

All the time back in Erroll's uncle's car I wondered what made me kiss Alan like that. It must have been madness. I'd never get him off my back now. On the other hand, he was a nice boy. I felt a bit sorry for Erroll coming all the way to Joburg just to see me, but as I told him in the car, there's lots of dishy girls in Grahamstown.

Anyhow, that's when things started to get intense with Alan. When I gave him the go-ahead at that party to phone me, I didn't realize he would phone me every day for an hour. After nearly a month of it, I was getting fed up.

6

I really liked Alan, but he was very possessive. He wanted me all for himself, like a stingy kid with a Peppermint Crisp. But he did unexpected things.

On the first morning of term, I was standing at the school gate with Merle and a few other friends watching this new Form I girl arrive in a cream-colored, chauffeur-driven Jaguar. The girl was pretty, with long blond pigtails.

"I'll be here one forty-five P.M., Miss Glenda," the black chauffeur called out. He was wearing a white and navy-blue peaked cap, which he was very proud of because he kept adjusting it.

"School only finishes at ten to two."

"I'll be early, Miss Glenda," he said, as the Jaguar purred off down the road.

Glenda marched confidently into her new school, leaving me and my friends murmuring about spoiled Joburg bitches. Anyhow, soon after that, Alan's younger sister, Donnay, turned up. She was too young to be at high school, she told us, but she was on her way to her primary school.

"So what brings you here, Donnay?" I asked her.

"I've got something for you from Alan," she said cutely, her two bunny-teeth sticking out of her mouth.

As she gave me this parcel with a ribbon round it all my classmates went "Ooooooo! Who's the boy?" It was none of their business, and I refused to open the package with them looking.

"Say thank you to him for me, Donnay, will you?"

"Yes," she said. "And I'll give him a kiss," she added, laughing and running off, her pigtails bouncing like mad.

When I opened the package later, I found this seed necklace inside with a letter all in beautiful handwriting, saying things like "To my dear Ruth." The letter was slushy, and I didn't like slush, but the necklace was nice if you liked necklaces. I didn't. I never wore them.

On the phone, Alan asked me out to see this play at a church somewhere in Parktown. It was difficult to say no, after I'd accepted his present.

We went with his mate Merv and his girlfriend Adele. Merv was eighteen, a year older than Alan, and therefore had a driving license. He also had the use of his father's van.

This van was always piled high with merchandise. His father supplied medicines and cosmetics to chemists and stores that traded with Africans. So Alan and I had to share the back of the van with boxes of Triple Action Kurra Powders, with its three active ingredients; Lewis's BB Tablets, which the African Mr. Transvaal takes for power; Karroo Beauty Cream for African women, because you know how our South African sun darkens a girl's skin; and Ambi Special, the best skin-lightener in the world, only eighty-seven cents per large tube. The only real problem was Merv's obsession with Adele. They spent the whole night smooching, except for when he needed both hands on the wheel to take a corner.

The play was pretty good. It was about these two Africans called Di-di and Go-go who were waiting for a chap called Godot to turn up. They were so bored with life that Di-di even tried to commit suicide from a tree, but the branch broke. Eventually someone did turn up, but it was only this giant African called Pozzo. He walked around with this albino black man on a chain like a dog, who was his servant and had to do everything he said. The albino's name was Lucky.

The actors were so close to us their spit sprayed over the audience, and I was glad we weren't in the front row because they got intermittent showers.

On the way home, Merv drove us up Linksfield Ridge and stopped there to have a good view of the northern suburbs. Actually, Merv wasn't interested in any view— except the view of Adele's mouth that he got with his tongue.

Alan and I were in the back of the van, and Merv expected big things of his friend, so Alan put his arm around my neck and fingered the seed necklace that he'd given me. I got goose bumps down my arms and legs. He was very nice to me and kissed me passionately and all that, and all the time his arm stayed around my neck, hanging over the top of my dress.

Eventually, I got a bit nervous that his hand was thinking of going on a voyage of discovery, so I made an excuse about wanting to get some fresh air. Actually, that was an understatement about saying I was nervous. I was petrified!

Fortunately, Alan didn't put up a fuss, and we walked up a path where on one side we had a view of the crisscrossing streetlights of Orange Grove stretching all the way to Sydenham and beyond toward the Joburg Drive-In, and on the other side we could see Cyrildene and the lit-up buildings of the city center. It was quiet except for the noise of cicadas and crickets, and the stars shone down on us in their millions, like more swarms of insects. The only ones I recognized were the Southern Cross blazing away somewhere above Turffontein. It was fantastic standing halfway between the earth and the sky with Alan holding on to me like I was his anchor.

When we climbed back in the van, Merv was disappointed with Alan for not getting more intimate with me, I could tell. For some reason, Merv thought he was Dr. Kinsey, the one who did the Kinsey Report about sex, and that he could solve everyone else's problems.

"Who the hell was Godot anyway?" he asked. "The bloke didn't even show up in the play."

"Maybe Godot is the thing everyone is waiting for in their lives," Alan said, and it sounded good to me.

"We have a philosopher in our midst," Merv said, with a good dose of sarcasm thrown in.

"Don't you think there's a connection of some sort between God and Godot?" Alan persisted.

"Definitely," Merv said. "Just like the connection between Pozzo and pizza."

The van swerved like mad down the hairpin bends, and I was glad we were still alive when we reached King David School at the bottom.

7

Mom wasn't too keen on my going out with Alan. The first time she set eyes on him, she thought he wasn't Jewish and that made her mad. But even when I told her he was, she couldn't get the idea out of her head.

"You know what happened to Jill Greenblatt on Fifth Avenue?"

I knew. Mom had told me five hundred thousand times.

"I know what happened, Mom."

"Well, then you'll know that her parents are still saying prayers for her as if she was dead. She married a non-Jew and that's what resulted. So don't ever think of doing that to me."

"His family's Jewish, I tell you."

"His name sounds Afrikaans to me," Mom said, closing her eyes and shaking her head, probably adding her own quick prayer for Jill Greenblatt.

When she discovered that Alan's father ran a small men's clothing shop on Louis Botha Avenue, she wasn't exactly thrilled.

"They must be destitute, poor people. You should have found out first."

I hated Mom for being a snob about people. I mean, boys you went out with ought to be intelligent and all that, but I didn't think they needed to be that rich.

"They're not that badly off," I said. "They've got a tennis court at their house. We haven't."

Mom was probably about to think up some other criticism, so I produced my trump card.

"Did I tell you that Alan is studying medicine?" I said, knowing doctors and lawyers were highest on my mom's list of marriageable professions.

"Oh, why don't you say so in the first place?" Mom said. "Why don't you invite him over for dinner? He can come on Wednesday, and Emily can cook us some roast lamb."

I suppose Mom was trying to be friendly in her own way. Also, no doubt, it would give her the chance to investigate for herself if he was Jewish or not. In any event, I should have known it wasn't a good idea to invite him over.

Mannie was really on form that night. He rang his little silver bell for John to bring in the soup course. John was garden boy during the day, but at mealtimes he was more like a waiter, wearing a little white apron.

No sooner had John brought the soup and returned to the kitchen, than Mannie rang the bell again.

"Yes, Master?"

"Look at this mark on the spoon!" Mannie yelled.

"Sorry, Master, I get another one."

"Why doesn't Emily wash it properly?"

"I don't know, Master. I will ask her."

"She should check all the cutlery before putting it on the table," Mannie raged.

"Yes, Master."

John brought Mannie a new spoon, shining it with a white cloth all the way from the kitchen to the dining room.

I was so embarrassed. Mannie and John reminded me so much of Pozzo and Lucky. Only thing missing was the chain around John's neck. I caught Alan's eye and tried to apologize somehow. He gave me a gentle, understanding smile. I bet that didn't happen at his house.

"I hear your brother is a politician," Mannie said to Alan.

Alan laughed. "Not quite a politician. But he is studying politics at Wits."

"Is he a communist?" Mannie said, smiling falsely.

"Mannie!" Mom said. "It's none of our business, really."

"I was just asking politely," Mannie said. Polite, my foot!

"I don't mind the question," Alan said. "He's not a communist, but he's read a lot about it. I think he's more of a socialist or a humanitarian."

"Not much difference between them all!" Mannie said. "And what are your beliefs?"

"He doesn't study politics," I butted in.

"I've just started medicine. But if you mean my personal beliefs, I suppose I'm a liberal-minded person."

"Not that much difference between liberalism and communism either," Mannie said, shlurping his soup. Typical Mannie. The only differences he ever noticed were between one-rand and five-rand notes.

Lenore sat opposite Alan and me. I noticed her checking

out Alan every now and again. No doubt she was curious to see what sort of a boy fancied me. She had no shortage of boyfriends, that's for sure. Nearly every day, some boy or other walked her home from school, and she was quite keen on this one boy, Hilton, who took her out most Saturday nights.

"So what kind of doctor are you going to be?" Mannie asked.

"Obstetrician, I think," Alan said.

"Is there much money in that?" Mannie asked, ringing the silver bell, because he'd finished his soup.

"I don't know. I'm just interested in the process of birth."

"Is this brisket?" Mannie said, sniffing at his plate like a dog. "You know I don't like lamb."

Poor Alan. I should never have asked him round.

"Your one isn't lamb," Mom said. "It's brisket. Emily prepared it especially for you."

"Smells like lamb," Mannie said. "Must have been cooked together." He rang the silver bell again. "John, go ask Emily if she cooked the brisket and the lamb together."

"Yes, Master."

John looked so humble walking in and out of that dining room with his shiny dark skin and his starchy white apron, but I often thought if he got juiced up one night with kaffirbeer he'd come storming in with the garden fork like a wild Zulu, ring Mannie's little bell, and let him have it through those bloated guts of his.

But he never complained, not even once in the eight years since Mannie had been living there.

"She says she cooked it separately, Master."

"Smells like lamb."

"No, Master."

"Tell me, Alan," Mom butted in, trying in her way to relieve the tension, "is Gerber an Afrikaans name?"

8

I must tell you about my mom. You know, she wasn't always so bad. Before she married Mannie she was sometimes sad, but never neurotic.

I think the sadness dated from the time my real dad died. Of course, I was too young to know what she was like before that. But his death knocked the wind out of her sails. It must have been tragic, that's for sure—they were only married for five years. Mom never talked much about it, just to say that he had died in a drowning accident in Natal.

To me it seemed like she held on to her sadness and wouldn't let it go. Perhaps it was all she had left of my real dad. And she would hardly ever listen to music.

We didn't own a hi-fi, and the small radio was only ever used for the news and horse-racing results, or for the *Surf Show Pickabox*, or for *Consider Your Verdict*, which Mom listened to regularly. Sure, we had a piano, but Mom hardly ever played it, and when she did, she only played the opening of the "Moonlight" Sonata, and then tears would roll from each eye down her hollowed-out cheeks. It's not that she didn't laugh sometimes, because she did. But under the laugh you could hear the pain.

Even the servants didn't listen to the Bantu radio if

Mom was home, which was unusual in our neighborhood, to say the least. I don't think Mom had ever asked the servants not to play music in her hearing, but more likely they just knew that music was a no-no. Of course, they played loud music in their servants' quarters behind the house.

But before Mannie came we had some good times. In those days Lenore and I used to get on just fine—in fact, we were best friends—and Granny used to live with us. I think the best time we ever had together was our trip to the Victoria Falls.

It was Uncle Barney's idea, that's Mom's favorite brother. He arranged the whole trip for her and bought the tickets and said Granny could stay with him and Aunt Helen. I even think he paid part of the money for that trip. He insisted that Mom have a holiday. "Otherwise you're going to have a nervous breakdown, and then who'll look after your children? You've got to put things behind you," he told her, "and start again."

We sat for three hours at the Victoria Falls, Lenore and Mom and me, and we stared at the cascading water. I don't know about Mom and Lenore, but I know that I got completely lost in the movement of that water. If you haven't ever been to the Victoria Falls it's difficult to understand how a person could get lost in those waters. But it's so magnificent! Please God, one day I'll go there again, and if I have children, I'll take them to see what a wonder it is.

We had a picnic lunch there, watching the misty rainbows hovering in the gorge, and after lunch we crossed to the other side and spent three more hours just sitting and staring. It was so beautiful. Lenore was good as gold. It's a magic place, I'm sure of it.

I don't think I ever felt so close to Mom as that day. She hugged Lenore and me closely, as if we were both very precious to her.

A strange thing happened, though, at the hotel in Bulawayo. I broke the mirror in my vanity case.

Mom and Lenore were downstairs in the hotel lounge at the time, and, oh my God, was I worried about her finding the broken mirror when she returned. You see, it was her superstitious beliefs that caused the trouble. "If you break a mirror, you have seven years of bad luck." I was desperate to save her worrying about me for seven long years, so I staged a burglary to explain the breakage.

I strewed clothes from all our traveling suitcases all over the room and spilled the contents of Mom's handbag on the floor. And I took the twenty-two rand that were in her purse and hid them under the carpet of the hotel staircase.

Then I rushed down into the lounge and said, "Mom, we've been burgled."

There was a huge kerfuffle, and the manager came to our room to inspect the burglary.

"I better call the police," he said.

"Don't worry," my mom said. "They only seem to have taken the money from my purse. Nothing else is missing and, thank God, we're all of us unharmed."

"And they broke the mirror in my vanity case," I added.

"Oh, never mind about your vanity case," Mom said.

That money is probably still there under the hotel carpet. When I go back to the Falls one day I may even take a peek to see if it's still there after all these years.

When we got back to Joburg after that holiday, Mom was in much better spirits. And she did decide to start a new life. But she should have known better than to start a new life with Frank Emmanuel Hirsch! My way of looking at it was that *he* was the seven years of bad luck I got for breaking that mirror.

He wasn't a doctor or a lawyer, so my mom getting involved with him should have been against her own principles. But she never saw it like that. She was so overwhelmed by his flatteries that she only saw his wealth.

He was rich as sin, I'll grant that. There was even a trading estate near one of the townships that was named after him: Hirschville. The estate wasn't really named after him—he gave it that name himself. He bought the land years and years ago, developed it, and made a fortune.

As soon as they were married, everything changed. Within a year, Granny was in the Old Aged Home where she died, and everything in our house became a stupid routine.

Before he came, only music was taboo. But after his arrival, all noise was taboo. Why? Because His Royal Highness liked to sleep in silence, that's why. And he slept all hours of the day and night. He didn't have to work regular hours. His property business in town ran so smoothly, he only needed to check up every now and again that his partner Ullman had pulled off some deal, or other. Which meant he was home a lot of the time, and whenever he hung a sock over his bedroom-door handle, we all had to tiptoe around the place, whispering to each other.

That's not all. He had rules about everything. Our two cocker spaniels weren't allowed in the house anymore because they dropped hairs everywhere; Lenore and I weren't allowed to bring friends home unless we arranged it in advance; we weren't allowed in the lounge when he and Mom were playing bridge with the Greenbaums; we weren't ever allowed in the main bedroom where he and Mom slept; we had to be seated at dinner at five-thirty exactly; etc., etc.

Over the years Mannie lived in our house things had been getting worse and worse. He grated my liver, and I couldn't stand the sight of him anymore.

There was always something that irritated him. For example, Alan's phone calls.

"You can only use the phone after six o'clock," Mannie said to me after I'd put down the phone.

"Who said?"

"I said."

"It's not your phone," I said.

"Oh, whose is it then?"

"It's Mom's. She pays for it."

"And don't I contribute?" Mannie said, looking offended. "You should ask your mother who pays for the phone around here. Anyway, Ullman can't get through to me if you're on the phone for hours."

"I never speak for hours."

"Oh don't you? I timed you today. Sixty-five minutes."

"That's not hours. That's one hour and five minutes. Who gave you the right to time me in my own house?"

"It's my house, too. I'm married to your mother, don't forget!"

"How can I ever forget?"

"You're a troublemaker, you know that, Ruth? A troublemaker. Ever since I came to live here you've tried to drive a wedge between your mother and me. But it won't work. I'm here to stay. If you don't like it, you'll be the one who leaves, not me."

"I'm going to tell Mom that you're threatening me."

"Go ahead. Tattletale! Go on. Go upset your mother!"

I didn't let him see me crying. I ran to my room, shut the door, and only then let the tears out. I put my nightie in my mouth to stop me screaming.

It was reaching that point where the house was too small for the both of us.

9

Most nights, after Mannie had retired to sleep, Mom and I used to have a heart-to-heart in the breakfast room. It was called the breakfast room, but really it should have been called the telephone room, or maybe the study, because nobody ever ate there. It had been the breakfast room before Mannie arrived in the house and decided that the proper place for breakfast was in the dining room.

In the old days these chats with Mom used to be friendly, but since Mannie came on the scene they had deteriorated into moan sessions.

"I just can't put up with Mannie's nonsense anymore," I told her. "He's disgusting."

"I'm sorry you haven't got a real father. He was so good to you, Ruth. You couldn't do a thing wrong in his eyes. But it's not my fault the way things turned out!" she said.

"I didn't say it was," I said. "But if only you hadn't married Mannie."

"I married him partly for you, you know."

I did know. She had drummed it into me so often.

"I wanted you to have a father around the house during your teenage years. But I also married him because I was lonely and he was nice to me. And to you. Don't you remember he used to bring you Flakey's and Milky Bars? And he used to take me out dancing and to bioscope."

"Mom, that was a long time ago. He hasn't done anything nice for you, or for me, in years. Besides, he wouldn't part nowadays with the money for a Milky Bar. He just lies around all day. It's damn embarrassing."

"No need to start swearing, young lady!" she said, raising her voice.

"That's not swearing," I said. "It's him or me. I can't stand it anymore."

"Can't you be nice to him, Ruthie? For my sake at least. Look how nicely Lenore gets on with him."

It was true. Lenore never bothered about Mannie. She wasn't fond of him, she told me that, but she didn't hate him either. Maybe it's because she never remembered our real dad, whereas I did. I was four when he passed away, but she was only two. Maybe that made all the difference.

10

When Mannie moved into our house, he brought seven wooden figurines with him. Of these, the most impressive was the witch doctor, who wore only a miniature lionskin around his waist. On his head he wore a buckskin headdress with two feathers stuck in it. He was in a squatting position, using a pounding stick and mixing bowl.

The other six figures were: a muscular warrior holding a metal assegaai; a pipe smoker; a drummer with a real skin drum; a female dancer; a young girl carrying a water jug on her head; and a woman with a baby on her back. These females were proud because of their large breasts and pointed nipples. It's a known fact that African women have larger breasts than whites, and the sculptor had made the most of this fact, using the grain of the wood, like contours on a map, to emphasize the fleshy hills.

Those seven carvings stood on the mantelpiece in all their nakedness, but like all cheap tourist trash bought while on holiday somewhere, nobody ever took much notice of them. They just lived out their lives in boring, white lounges all over the country.

From my seat at the dining table I had a good view of them, and I could see them watching us, especially on Friday nights when Mom lit the candles and Mannie held up his silver goblet of wine to sing Kiddush like a tone-deaf parrot.

It was only John who ever touched them. Once a week he had to dust them and give them a rub with Pride furniture polish until their blackness gleamed.

11

Apart from those seven wooden figurines, Mannie brought very little to our house, I can tell you. Only a telephone table which sat in the breakfast room, one armchair, a bedroom rug, and, oh yes, the ivory tusk—the valuable ivory tusk—carved into a row of little elephants holding each other's tails with their trunks. That was it! Mind you, our house was fully furnished, and we had difficulty even finding places for those rubbish items that he did bring.

He brought these objects from his previous house, where he'd lived fifteen years with his wife, before she divorced him. I always hoped it wouldn't take fifteen years before Mom got smart.

He contributed so little to the house. But a year or two after Mannie married Mom, he did make one alteration to the house at his own expense. He put up a railing round the bath and hung a plastic curtain down from it. You could see blurry shapes through that plastic, but not details.

I never used that curtain. Whenever I had a bath, I locked the door and that was that. And I don't think Mom or Lenore ever used it either. It was only Mannie who did. You know why? He was so damn idle that he just lay in the bath for hours on end sometimes. God alone knows what he was doing in there. Maybe reading the share prices or studying the horses. But I had serious doubts.

He'd be in that bath behind that plastic curtain every morning when Lenore and I needed to wash before school. I'm convinced he timed it specially. I would just brush my teeth as quickly as possible and give my face a wipe-down with a damp cloth, then go back to my room to brush my hair. All the time I kept my eyes away from that plastic curtain, just in case I'd see something through it. It was truly revolting to be in the same room with his great wobble of flesh all naked behind there, smelling of bath oil. And like I said before, God knows what he was doing in there. Sometimes I'd hear soapy noises like he was rubbing himself. I just hoped he had a cleanliness obsession and that the noise was him washing.

Sometimes he'd even call John.

"Bring me a mango, John!"

And John had to bring a mango on a plate with a knife and put it on the corner of the bath. It disgusted me. God only knows what John thought of it. But he never complained.

"And take away those clippings also!"

The clippings were Mannie's toenail clippings, piled neatly on the bottom corner of the bath. John always scooped them into his hands and took them out of the bathroom.

Naturally I often wondered if Mannie got his kicks out of being naked there with other people being in the room. It was either that or extreme idleness. Either way it made my flesh creep. It was something I ignored when I was younger, but I couldn't stand it anymore.

"You have to stop Mannie using the bathroom in the mornings," I said to Mom.

"He likes his morning bath," Mom said, hardly even looking up from typing out some legal documents. Mom worked hard at Zlotkin & Hillowitz during the day, and at night she did extra private work.

"Mom, listen to me! I'm sixteen now and it's not right. This morning his plastic curtain wasn't even properly shut."

"I'm sure it must have been," Mom said.

"Do you think I'm lying?" I asked. "You can ask John. He had to put the mango right at the corner where it wasn't shut properly. You ask him."

"It must have been a mistake," Mom said.

"Mom, it's horrible. This used to be our house. But now we can hardly move in it without his perversions."

I used that word specially because I knew it would get a reaction from Mom. She looked up from her typing.

"How dare you say that? He may be bone idle, but he's not perverted. You can't just accuse . . ."

"Look Mom, I can't take it anymore. I'm going to do something terrible if you don't change things around here. He's like an old horse, with that great stomach of his."

"Stop it, Ruth!" Mom cried.

12

It was a scorching summer that year. It hadn't rained for ages. Some of the pavements outside our house were so parched, the rusty dry earth cracked open like the thick skin on the heels of some barefoot person. The rivers were drying up, and there were warnings that you could catch bilharzia if you swam in infested water.

The dryness was like a blotting paper that sucked the sense out of people's brains, I'm sure of it. There were Christian priests who proclaimed that God was withholding the rain as a means of chastising people, and that only if the faithful would pray would the rain fall. "The Word of God most distinctly said that only God could give rain. Our prayers will definitely help."

It was John who felt the drought most, because it was difficult to make the garden look good with everything shriveling in the intense heat. He had to hose the garden every evening and move the sprinkler around the lawn all day just to keep the grass green. Even so, the lawn was thinning out in places and turning that awful dusty yellow.

13

One night I had one of my hysterical outbursts.

Alan had popped in to visit me after he got back from varsity. We were sitting in the lounge, just talking, when Mannie came out of his bedroom in a stinking mood. He was in his dressing gown, and he walked right past us on his way to the kitchen without so much as saying hello to either of us.

On the way back he stopped and said to me, "You've got a damn cheek to complain behind my back to your mother!"

I was furious that he spoke to me like that in front of Alan.

"I like a bath every day," he said. "My bath is none of your damn business!"

I let his comments pass because I was so ashamed in front of Alan. But later that night my head was white-hot with rage.

"I'm ashamed to have my friends here," I said to Mom. I poured out a stream of complaints against Mannie. "And he was in his pajamas and gown at four in the afternoon. He's so disgusting and so crude."

Mom defended him.

"He's lazy, but he doesn't mean any harm."

"Doesn't he? He just wants his own way all the time. And he wants you to pamper him. I don't know how you manage to sleep in the same room with him."

"That's none of your business, Ruth!"

"Sis, Mom. It's disgusting!" I was out of control. I wanted to shake Mom and make her change her ways. I screamed at her instead. "You should get rid of him!"

"Stop it, Ruth! I know it was a mistake. What can I do?"

Mom started crying and Lenore came rushing in.

"What's going on, Mom?" she asked. Lenore really got on my nerves sometimes. She always tried to calm things down, but really she just couldn't endure confrontation—even when the issue concerned her own well-being.

"It's nothing, darling," Mom sniveled.

"It's not nothing," I screamed to Lenore. "Why don't you say what you really think of him. Tell Mom what you told me!"

Lenore had told me a while back that she wished Mom had never met Mannie.

But she didn't say a thing. Instead, she put her arm around Mom's neck and looked at me timidly. Before I could stir up her feelings, Mannie came rushing in.

"Is she starting her nonsense again?" he said, without even mentioning my name. "You're aggravating your mother, you know that? Every night you scream at her. You've got no consideration for others."

"Oh, and you have, I suppose?"

"You need to be taught a lesson!" he said.

"Go ahead!" I said. "Just you try!"

"Stop it, for God's sake, you two!" Mom screamed.

"It never used to be like this before he came!" I screamed.

"Get out of here!" Mannie shouted.

The white-heat in my head started to blank out my common sense. I turned to the wall and started to pummel it with my fists.

"Stop your hysterics!" Mannie shouted. He got that word from my mom. She always called my tantrums "hysterics," ever since I could remember.

Through my tears I saw the three of them standing there, united in their anger against me.

I went to my bedroom and made plans.

14

The next morning, as usual, Mannie was in the bath behind the plastic curtain when I went in to brush my teeth. I held my breath, brushed my teeth, and ran out of the bathroom, releasing my breath in the passage.

I waited for Mom to go off to work. Then I told Lenore to cycle to school on her own. I packed a suitcase full of my clothes and I walked out of the house, up Noreen Avenue to catch the bus.

John must have seen me leaving and told Emily. She came running up the road.

"Where you going, Rootie? Your mother is going to cry. Please come back!"

"No, Emily. I must go."

PART TWO

1

I GOT AS FAR AS UNCLE BARNEY'S HOUSE
in Cyrildene. He and Helen welcomed me and gave me a
cup of sweet tea and some Romany Creams. "After a bad
experience you need something sweet," Helen said. They
told me I could certainly stay the night or even a few days,
but only on condition I let my mom know where I was and
that I was safe.

So what could I do? I had to phone her, and she cried
and cried and begged me to come home.

I spent the night talking to Uncle Barney and Aunt
Helen, and they were amazingly sympathetic. I didn't tell
them intimate details, but they seemed to know all about
Mannie's peculiarities.

"He's a difficult man," Barney said. "I can see it's not
easy for you, Ruth. But you'll have to find a way of exist-
ing in the same house as him, for a year at least, until you

finish matric. After that, when you go to university, you can live in the residence."

"I can't go back," I said. "Not unless there's a drastic change."

"Well, you must communicate to your mom and Mannie the conditions that are necessary for you to go on living there, and then see what they want from *you*. You may have to compromise a little, but see if you can reach some agreement."

"He's not like you, Uncle Barney. He's not a man you can reason with."

"I know he's difficult."

"We also find it hard to relate to him, don't we, Barney?" Aunt Helen said. "But we do it for your mom's sake."

"Well, I can't just live for my mom's sake. I'm also a person."

"Yes, Ruth, we understand," Helen said. "You can sleep in Edith's room. I keep it ready for her when she comes home for holidays. And please, make yourself comfortable. Just go into the kitchen whenever you want and help yourself! You're very welcome, and you can stay as long as you like. Until you feel ready to go back."

Edith's room had her ballet trophies proudly displayed in a cabinet and also a load of certificates on the wall. Aunt Helen showed me a scrapbook she kept about Edith's progress overseas, with photos of her performing in London.

I used to do ballet when I was younger and even performed in the Eisteddfod once. I had to do a classical ballet, a Spanish dance, an impromptu, and a demi-character called the Ice Maiden. But I gave it up when I got to high school. I wasn't talented like Edith, so it didn't seem worth the bother.

I didn't sleep too well in Edith's room. I was worried about how I'd hurt Mom by running away, I must admit.

First thing in the morning, she arrived. She hugged and kissed me, and thanked Barney and Helen for looking after me.

"Mom, I'm not coming back unless things change. Is that clear?"

"Yes, of course, Ruthie. Now hurry up, I don't want you to be late for school. I've written a note to say you had laryngitis yesterday."

So that was the extent of my little excursion. One night! And nothing changed. The next morning, as usual, Mannie was there in the bath behind the plastic curtain when I went in to brush my teeth. I held my breath, ran in, collected up my toothbrush and flannel, and took them into the kitchen.

2

It's true the Gerber family wasn't too wealthy. They lived in a sprawling, red-bricked house in a Sydenham back street. It was a large house with many rooms and two long passages at right angles to each other. At the bend in the passage were some steps leading to the one upstairs room, and at the far end of the passages was a glass door leading into a separate annex where Alan's grandparents lived.

The garden wasn't that big, because most of it was taken up with the so-called tennis court. Nobody could ever have played real tennis on that court, though, because its red sandy surface was badly cracked in most places, with grass and weeds poking through. The high fence round it was the only thing about that court that was still in good condition.

There were lots of people in the Gerber household. Besides the old grandparents, there was Alan's mom and dad, and his older brother Bobby, and Alan himself, and his younger sister Donnay who brought Alan's letters and presents to my school, and little Sam, who was only five years old.

The first time I visited there, Alan introduced me to his mom and dad. His mom was preparing salads for lunch and little Sam was driving her crazy.

"Ma, can I feed Oenk, Poenk, and Stoenk? Can I, Ma, please? Donnay did it yesterday. It's my turn today, Ma, please."

"Yes, Sam, just take a handful of food and get out of here."

Little Sam poured out crumbs from a cardboard tube and ran out.

"Are Oenk, Poenk, and Stoenk birds?" I asked.

"No, they're our three goldfish, out there in the pond. Do you want to go see them?" Alan asked.

"No, I don't like goldfish," I said. "They give me the creeps."

Their dog was a cheerful thing, though—a white, woolly mongrel, always wagging its tail, with a fringe over its eyes so it could hardly see where it was going. He couldn't stop licking me when I arrived.

"Down, Woodenhead!" Alan said repeatedly, but the dog didn't obey.

The Sunday meal was a braai in the garden. It was spread over three garden tables: the steak and chops and boerewors on one table, the salads on another, and the cold drinks, beer, and wine on the third.

Just before lunch, Alan's mate Steve turned up for a visit, and he was persuaded to stay for the braai by Mrs. Gerber. Mr. and Mrs. MacGibbon, some friends of the family, turned up unexpectedly during lunch, and even though they'd already eaten, they indulged in the desserts.

Alan's grandparents emerged from their annex and also joined in with the meal. The old man had Parkinson's—you could tell by the tremor in his hands, especially when he reached for food, and also his tongue kept up a continuous licking of his lips.

"Sakabona!" he said to me.

"Sakabona!" I said back to him, hoping that was what he expected of me.

"Sakabona fish!" he said, giggling to himself. To this day I don't know what's funny about mixing an African greeting and a fish, but he found it funny.

Alan's brother Bobby was great-looking. He reminded me a bit of Alan Bates from *Zorba the Greek*, except that he didn't speak with a posh accent.

"How old's Bobby?" I asked Alan.

"It's easy to work out the ages in our family," Alan said, "because my mom and dad suffer from the six-year itch."

"What's that?"

"There's six years between each of us children."

"So Bobby's twenty-three," I calculated.

"Have some more ice cream," Mrs. Gerber said to me. "With a figure like yours you don't need to diet."

I didn't know whether she meant it as a compliment or

not, but Alan smiled across at me, so I took it well.

"I was telling Ruth about your six-year itch," Alan teased. "You're due for another baby this year, Ma. Are you pregnant yet?"

Mrs. Gerber laughed.

"No more babies for me. You lot are enough of a handful. What do you say, Violet? Haven't I got enough children?"

Violet was their servant and had come to clear away the dirty plates.

"Heh-heh, Madam," Violet cackled. "Madam is still too young. Madam can have plenty more babies."

"Here, Violet, this is for you."

Mrs. Gerber gave Violet one plate with steak, chops, and boerewors on it, and another plate with a large portion of fruit salad and ice cream.

"Thank you, Madam."

For sure, if this had been our house, the servant would not have got the same food as the white people ate. My mom gave John and Emily special servants' meat. Leftovers of our meals were kept carefully in the fridge for another day.

After lunch, Alan asked me if I liked Mahler's Second Symphony. I didn't even know Mahler's First Symphony. In fact, I had never heard of Mahler.

Alan placed two cushions on the royal-blue carpet midway between the two loudspeakers, and we lay beside each other listening to the music.

The music was very powerful, I must admit. Listening to it was a new experience for me. I hardly knew any classical music. It was angry, emotional, deep, but also at times sweet, tender, gentle.

"It's called the Resurrection Symphony."

"Is it Christian music?" I asked.

"No. It's not any religion. Just Mahler pondering on the meaning of his life."

"What did he find?" I asked.

"He found this music, for a start," Alan said.

Halfway through the music, Mr. Gerber called us out. He had arranged this cricket game on the tennis court. Him and Bobby were captains, and they chose two teams. Bobby chose Steve and me and Mrs. Gerber. Mr. Gerber chose his friend Mac, and Mrs. MacGibbon as well, and Alan and Donnay. Little Sam wasn't chosen, but just before he started crying, Bobby said we'd have him on our side, because he was a number one batsman and he could bat first.

"Are you coming to play, General?" Mr. Gerber teased his father.

The old man did have the bearing of a warrior, which was probably why he was referred to as the general.

"Leave me in peace!" he said.

Little Sam was out first ball, but they gave him a few more chances. Eventually he was caught and bowled by Mac, but he wouldn't leave the crease.

"It was a no-ball!" he shouted.

"How can you say it was a no-ball?" Mr. Gerber asked.

"He bowled too fast," Sam said.

"Come on, Sammy," Bobby said. "You've given our side a seven-runs start. That's really good."

"I made eight runs," Sam said.

"Yes, that's right, eight runs," Bobby said. "Now give somebody else the bat."

"I'm not out," Sam said.

Mr. Gerber walked up to little Sam and forced the bat out

of his hand. Little Sam started howling and marched off.

"It's not fair! You're all bortzekant!" he screamed, as he disappeared up the gangway into the house.

"What's bortzekant?" I asked Alan.

"Search me," Alan said. "That kid lives in a world of his own."

I never played cricket before, and I couldn't bat to save my skin, but it was good fun trying. I was given three innings before I was declared out.

"That was good, Ruth!" Bobby encouraged me. "You gave it a good slog!"

When the blokes batted I kept out of the way because they hit so hard. Even though it was a tennis ball it would have hurt me like mad, so I didn't even try.

"You should have dived for that one!" Bobby shouted, laughing at me.

But the funniest batsman was Steve. When he went into bat, he brushed his hair and adjusted his peaked cap.

"You're not going dancing, Steve!" Mr. Gerber teased.

"It's my lucky cap," Steve said. "I scored eighty-five for the club last Saturday wearing this cap."

"He looks like Joe Potz with noodles," Alan's grandfather said from behind the fence. I didn't know who Joe Potz was, or what he was doing with the noodles, but the general obviously found Steve's hat amusing.

The first ball Steve slogged right out of the tennis court for six—he's got very powerful wrists—and Woodenhead was only too happy to retrieve the ball for us. (That dog spent the whole afternoon running around the outside of the fence, hoping he'd be called to join in the game.) But the second ball hit Steve somewhere round the knees.

"LBW!" Alan shouted.

Mr. Gerber raised his forefinger, which meant out.

"No way, man!" Steve grumped. "It hit my thigh."

Mr. Gerber looked across at Mac who raised his forefinger as well.

"No way!" Steve said. "Look, here's the mark. It's above my knee."

"That was out, my boy!" Mr. Gerber insisted.

Steve shook his head and readjusted his lucky cap.

"Come on, Steve, give someone else a chance—go and join Sam."

Everyone except Steve laughed.

At that moment Sam came down the gangway again. He was carrying a suitcase with a shirtsleeve hanging out.

"And where are you off to, young man?" Mrs. Gerber asked.

"I'm going to Prumps!"

He marched down the drive to the gates. Woodenhead wanted to follow him, but Mr. Gerber called the dog back.

"Where's Prumps?" I asked Alan.

"Search me," Alan said.

Little Sam walked out onto the pavement, down past one house, and into the next. It was where his friend Trevor lived.

The cricket game continued until Mac ran into the fence and retired with a red diamond pattern impressed into his forehead. I think our team won.

Mrs. Gerber brought out tea and Cokes and Hubbly Bubbly and a huge chocolate cake. Bobby cut a piece off the cake and handed the small piece around while he pretended to keep the big piece all for himself.

During the tea break Mr. Gerber suddenly jumped up out of his deck chair screaming, "Get the gun, Alan!"

What did he want a gun for? My God, I got a fright!—
until I saw him pointing at this locust which had landed
near his chair.

The gun was a rifle, and Mr. Gerber stalked the dangerous
beast until the point of his rifle was within six inches. He
pulled the trigger and blew the poor locust's head right off.

Alan whispered in my ear that his dad was paranoid
about locusts and lizards and snakes and insects. He also
whispered that he wanted to take me to his bedroom to
show me his medical books. What did I want to see medical books for, I'd like to know! His fingers found my fingers in the grass, and I suddenly realized that it wasn't
medical books he wanted to show me at all.

"Not now, Alan," I whispered back.

"Did you kiss her ear, Alan?" Donnay asked.

"No, I didn't actually," Alan said. "I asked her if
eleven-year-old sisters get on her nerves."

Mr. Gerber had no sooner settled down in his deck chair
after his hunting expedition than he felt this rasping on his
arm. He leapt out of the chair again, thinking it was another locust, but it was only Mrs. Gerber tickling him with
a bottlebrush twig. Everyone roared with laughter, except
Mr. Gerber himself.

Donnay in the meantime was trying to fit the locust's
head back onto its body.

"Sis!" Mrs. Gerber said. "That's pooffy!"

Donnay giggled like mad.

As I gulped my last bit of chocolate cake, I noticed little
Sam sneaking back into the house.

"Have you come back from Prumps?" Bobby asked.

"Yes! There was nobody there."

"Well, come and have some chocolate cake when you've

unpacked after your long journey," Mrs. Gerber said.

Little Sam's escape to Prumps had been no more successful than my running away to Barney and Helen's.

Later, when little Sam had cheered up and his mouth was mushy with chocolate cake and Coke, Bobby felt it was safe to mention the cricket again.

"You scored a lot more than Steve, you know."

Little Sam smiled.

"You can borrow my hat if you like next week," Mr. Gerber said to Steve, who was scowling like mad.

When six o'clock came and it was time to go home, I was very reluctant to leave. I didn't want to go back to my house—it reminded me of this house around the corner from us that burned down when I was a kid. For days afterward I used to walk past that house to smell the ashes and look at the burnt objects in all the rooms. Some of the beds still had their shape, so did other bits of furniture, but if you hit them with a stick, they just crumbled. That's what my house was like. It had the shape of a family house, but if you had hit it with a stick, that shape would have just crumbled.

To me it seemed the Gerber household had a good, strong shape to it. I didn't want to go home that night. I may not have been in love with Alan, but I loved his family.

3

I enjoyed going out with the crew, even if it was just a ride into Hillbrow.

The crew were Alan, Merv, Steve, and Cyril. They were

all first-year medical students, except for Cyril who was doing dentistry, and they had been friends right through high school.

Merv's father's van could hold a lot of people when it wasn't full, but Merv drove too fast. Eighty miles an hour was nothing for him. The van swayed around from side to side, and the passengers were in grave danger of being concussed by Dr. Mackenzie's Venoids with its diuretic action, whatever that was, or by Zambuk, the world's best-known, most-valued first-aid treatment for all skin troubles, or by Brooklax, the laxative that gave you more energy, more strength, and more brain power.

Besides having a high opinion of his own cricketing skills, Steve really thought he was God's gift to women. I must admit he was cute-looking, with very blond hair and an appealing, rebellious expression just like James Dean. Actually he looked a lot like James Dean, except that he was taller and skinnier. He had no difficulty getting girl-friends, but he never went out with one girl more than two or three times.

On this one occasion he was with a girl called Carol, but he ignored her almost totally and spent the time combing his hair instead. He had a bottle of Gordon's Dry with him, which he made a great show of passing around, as though he were a big drinker. The other blokes had a swig or two, but Steve looked like he was having one too many.

Cyril was with this girl called Rhona, who had a big reputation, if you know what I mean—watermelon size. Excuse me for being bitchy, but she was known as the cheapest kugel around. She was actually the twin sister of Ezra Tabatznik, and he had failed Form 4 twice, so you can imagine what she was like. Most people said that those twins practiced sex on each other, and I wouldn't have been the least bit surprised.

I don't know what Cyril wanted with Rhona: he was a refined chap, always well dressed, with a polite and pleasant manner and an Ipana toothpaste smile. His father was a big surgeon in Joburg. Cyril didn't have to tell us: we all knew that his father knew Dr. Chris Barnard who did heart transplant operations in Cape Town.

After a vote to decide where to go—Merv wanted the Tadpole, Cyril fancied going to Nitebeat—we landed up at the Milky Way to avoid an argument.

Most of us had grape slush specials, and we took our time sucking up the purple, creamy liquid through thick straws.

As we were heading back to the van, I overheard Merv whispering to Alan.

"She likes you, man. I can tell. And Adele says so too. She's never wrong."

Alan glanced my way, but I pretended to be looking in a shop window.

"You must take the plunge, man. In the back of the van you just put your hand on her tits. She'll let you, don't worry. Then get your hand under her bra. You've got to do it sometime, you know."

Typical Merv! His talking gave me the shivers. He thought a female was just a pair of boobs with legs.

"At least you know Ruth's nice," Merv said to Alan. "Do you remember that girl Joyce I took to Cinerama?" Merv was screwing up his face and shrugging his shoulders as if the memory of the girl was like having worms poured down his shirt. "I got under her bra easy enough, but there was nothing there, man! Flat as a pancake! That's the worst thing that can happen. Boy, did I take her home quickly after that."

Poor Joyce! But it made me cringe when I heard Merv talk like that, though my face didn't let on that I'd overheard the conversation.

On the way back, Steve finished off the last of the Gordon's Dry. He then promptly flaked out behind a box of Lavoris mouthwash, and later Merv had to stop for him to do a Gordon's Dry grape-slush vomit on the pavement. I don't think Carol was too enchanted with him.

Fortunately for me, Alan didn't take Merv's advice, thank goodness, because I'd have probably jumped right out of that moving van if he had. But his hand had this way of hanging over my shoulders that gave me the real goose bumps. He wasn't shy or anything; he was probably waiting for the perfect moment.

On the doorstep he gave me another meaningful kiss. I think the meaning was: you're mine for life, body and soul, till death us do part, and all the rest of it.

4

Inside I found Mom whimpering in the kitchen with Emily trying to comfort her. Ever since Mom's first marriage, Emily had been her servant. Emily remembered my real dad but never spoke to me about him.

I think in some ways Emily was Mom's best friend, though Mom would never have admitted it. I don't mean that she and Emily socialized together or anything like that, of course not, but whenever Mom was unhappy, who did she turn to? Not to me or Lenore or Uncle Barney or Aunt Bertha. And certainly not to Mannie! No, she always retreated to the kitchen to Emily's soft-spoken words.

I liked Emily too. When I was little I remember I used to call her into my room on a cold winter's morning. "Get my socks, Emily," I used to say. Then I would stick my feet out from under my blankets. "Put them on for me, please!" And Emily would slide a clean pair of school socks over my feet for me.

When I was dressed I used to ask her to comb my hair. She made such neat plaits and tied them with red ribbons. Afterward she always removed the hairs from my comb and made sure they went in the bin. "Bad people can hurt you if they find your hair," she told me.

For years she used to baby-sit Lenore and myself whenever Mom had to go somewhere, and we would talk with her in the kitchen. And it was Emily who cooked all our food. Every day after school there would be a meal waiting for Lenore and me in the kitchen when we got home, and a marbled sponge cake for us to have when friends came over.

Emily was a good listener, the sort of person who could listen to your problems and keep your secrets.

She was the only one who knew what Lenore and I had done to the goldfish, but she never told on us. Years ago these Japanese people moved into Lusikisiki—that's the name hanging on the pole four houses down from us. At first, we thought they were Chinese and had something to do with the fah-fee game, and we couldn't understand why nonwhites were allowed to live in a white suburb. But then Mom explained her theory that although Chinese were nonwhite, Japanese were whites because Japan traded with South Africa, so the government made all Japanese people honorary whites, and they could live where they liked.

But Lenore and I thought that honorary whites or not, they couldn't be very nice people because they didn't let us sit on their wall, so one night we collected up all these empties from the backyard. They were mostly family-sized Cokes, but there were also a few Piccalilli bottles and Oros empties. We collected them in a large hessian sack and then we crushed them with a large rock.

We knew the Japanese were out that night, so we sneaked into Lusikisiki and dumped all the broken glass in the small pond. We were so proud at not being caught, but the next day there were all these dead goldfish floating on that pond. It was terrible. All the neighbors, including Mom, went to have a look at the ghastly sight.

Lenore and I pretended we were busy. Nobody knew it was us, except for Emily. I don't know how she knew, but she came into my room holding Lenore's hand, and she said, "That was a bad thing you and Lenore did."

"What?" I said, playing innocent.

"You know, with the broken glass in the fish pond."

"It was Lenore's idea," I said.

"Shame, Rootie, you the older one. You must know better."

I begged her please not to tell anyone, and she never did, thank goodness.

The Japanese family sold their house soon after that, but I don't think it was only because of the pond incident. I think they got worse insults from the adults in the neighborhood.

Now that house is occupied by Doreen Marks who is a

friend of mine. It's still called Lusikisiki, but the pond has been sort of filled in and arum lilies grow in it, which goes to show how long Emily kept our secret.

That incident proved Emily was very trustworthy. No wonder Mom could discuss personal matters with her.

5

"It is not your fault, Madam," Emily was saying when I walked into the kitchen. "The master doesn't like Baas Harry."

Not many people liked Harry P-chinsky. He had made oodles of money by running a concession store for Africans on one of the gold mines. People used to say that because he dealt with Africans for so long, he forgot how to be with people of his own color. He was a very unsociable person, I must say, but one thing about him, he worshiped Aunt Bertha, who was Mom's sister.

All those years he worked out in the bundu, he was apparently only thinking of Bertha—he wanted her to have the life-style of a queen or a duchess or something. She now walked around with diamonds on her fingers the size of grapes.

"One day she'll have her fingers cut off by some tsotsi in the street," Mannie used to say, because he was jealous that Harry could afford such lavish diamond rings for his wife. I'm sure Mannie could have afforded to buy Mom such rings, but he was as stingy as a dry twig in the Kalahari.

Harry and Mannie hated each other. They each despised

the way the other had earned their money. But as if that wasn't enough, they had this enormous quarrel just before Mannie married Mom.

What happened was that Aunt Bertha had been sitting on a bus in Klerksdorp when she overheard two people talking about Mannie Hirsch. These two people were saying that Mannie had inflicted physical violence on his previous wife and that she divorced him because of it. But who could believe Aunt Bertha's stories? She had this knack of always sitting behind just the right people on the bus who just happened to know the most intimate details of some member of your family—even though that person lived hundreds of miles away.

Anyhow, Harry had mentioned the wife-beating to Mom, and Mom had asked Mannie what the grounds were for his divorce. He accused Aunt Bertha of stirring up a termite's nest of trouble, and Harry defended his wife who could do no wrong in his eyes.

In the end Harry and Aunt Bertha refused to come to Mom's wedding.

Mom cried all the way through her wedding. I know, because I had a front-row view. When Mannie lifted his foot to smash the glass, which was the final part of the wedding ceremony, Mom's sobbing could be heard all around the synagogue. That glass broke into thousands of pieces that could never be glued together again, and Mom looked like she felt the same way. Maybe people thought she was crying with happiness. I even assumed she was sad because she was remembering getting married to my dad.

Later, in the registry, she hugged me close to her body. Her dress felt smooth against my face, and I could hear her sobbing into my hair.

"I'm making a terrible mistake," she moaned. "Bertha was right to warn me. I'll regret this day all the rest of my life."

What a happy wedding that was! The first waltz at the reception was "I'll Be Loving You, Always," and Mom sniveled half the dance into a tissue, and Mannie kept saying "Smile! Everyone's watching you," so she spent the other half of the waltz with this false smile on her face.

Mom and Emily looked up as I walked into the kitchen. Emily took a step back from Mom as if she had been caught in a forbidden moment of intimacy with the white madam.

"What's wrong now?" I asked.

Mom held up an invitation card to a twentieth wedding anniversary.

"Bertha and Harry have invited us to their celebration, but Mannie won't go."

Later that evening I heard Mom and Mannie arguing about it again.

"Who can travel all that way?" he said to Mom.

"You travel all the way to Witbank to see your properties," she reminded him.

"That's different," he answered. "I go by train."

"Well, let's go by train, then," she said.

"But then we'd have to sleep over. We can't get a train back to Joburg the same night. And we can't sleep over in that man's house."

That man, of course, was Harry. Mannie never mentioned him by name.

"Mannie, you're being so difficult."

"Your car's not comfortable," he said to Mom. "It's old.

You should get a new one, then we won't have this problem."

I thought, what a cheek! He's complaining about Mom's car—why didn't he buy one himself? He knew how to drive all right, but he just liked to be driven everywhere. Putting his foot down on the accelerator and changing gears was far too much effort for him. But even if he didn't want to drive, the least he could do would be to contribute money toward a new car.

"You always go on about the car. I don't find it uncomfortable."

"It's the fumes. They catch my throat. There's always been something wrong with that car."

"You're the only one who ever notices it."

"It's the state of my throat. Can I help it?"

"It's not your throat. Why don't you admit that it's because of Harry that you won't go?"

"OK, I admit it. Happy now?"

Mannie had a sneering look on his face, like he despised every molecule of Mom's personality. He turned away in silence. Now he wouldn't speak to her for a few hours—it was always the same ploy. And she would have to smolder for hours and hours, perhaps right through the night, until he decided that she had been sufficiently punished for daring to offend him.

She picked up the phone and dialed Klerksdorp to tell Bertha that they wouldn't be coming to her anniversary party.

Bertha was very put out.

"It's Mannie, isn't it?" she said. "Simmy and Ethel are coming from Joburg, and Barney and Helen, and Dave and Bitty."

"You know Mannie won't drive with anyone else," Mom explained.

"That man is tormenting the life out of you," Bertha said. "Why don't you just come? Leave him there and come yourself."

"Please, Bertha. I'm sorry. I can't come to a party on my own. It will be shameful, and I'll never hear the end of it here."

"He's been no use to you, that man," she said. "If you don't come, I never want to see him again. Do you understand?"

Some people grow grudges the way other people grow pumpkins. And Bertha was a prize pumpkin-grower, I can tell you.

She was furious and slammed the phone down on Mom. Mom was crying her eyes out. I put my arms around her shoulder and wiped her glasses for her. She looked like a blind bat without them.

She sobbed and sobbed. There was no way of comforting her, even though I tried, and I stayed up with her into the early hours of morning.

6

The following week Mom traded in her old Renault and bought a brand new Zephyr 6. You can guess how much money Mannie contributed to its purchase. You got it—a big fat zero, the same shape as his bloated belly. The new car was a sort of sky-blue color and smelt of new upholstery. She took Mannie and Lenore and me for a drive past the Jewish Old Aged Home and around the golf course.

Mannie loved the new car, but he still refused point-blank to go to Bertha's wedding anniversary.

"You promised to go if I got the new car," Mom screamed, turning to Mannie with bloodshot eyes.

"Watch where you're driving, woman!" Mannie shouted out. "I never promised anything, and anyway, you needed a new car."

I don't know if Aunt Bertha's story about Mannie beating up his first wife was accurate or not. It's true I had never seen him raise an arm to Mom, but physical violence isn't the only kind of violence, is it?

I really wanted that man out of my life and out of my mother's life. I knew he hated my mother, except when he needed her. Then he buttered her up with pathetic compliments, and she fell for it, over and over and over again. I couldn't believe it.

"You did promise you'd go," I said. "I heard you."

"Don't you dare butt in!" he yelled at me. "This has got nothing to do with you!"

Lenore bit her lip. She hated arguments. She gazed out of the window pretending nothing of all this was going on. I pressed my finger into her thigh, trying to goad her into saying something, but she kept silent.

My mom resented the way Mannie broke his promise. I know she did. You could tell from the bitter tone of her voice. But she continued the same way as before, and on Tuesday night they kept their bridge appointment with the Greenbaums, because Mannie was a bridge fanatic.

God knows why she did it. I never knew a Wednesday morning when they were on speaking terms. Mannie had a memory for cards like a Kodak camera, and he never left off telling Mom which card she had played wrong.

But every Tuesday night she went off with him to the Greenbaums. When I was younger Emily used to baby-sit for Lenore and me, but more recently Mom just used to make sure that Emily was around. Her greatest fear was that Emily would go out and leave Lenore and me alone in the house with just John in his room.

"Mom, I'm nearly sixteen."

"Yes, but Zlotkin's got a case now where this woman was raped by the garden boy in front of her three-year-old child."

That was the trouble with having a mother who worked for solicitors—she got the most gruesome stories in all their gory details.

"Yes, Mom, but John has been with us three years, and he's very quiet."

"That's what you think, my girl," Mom said. "In this case at work the garden boy had been with the family seven years. I can't even bear to think of it. In front of the child, sis!"

"OK, Mom, don't get in a panic. The back door's locked, and Emily won't go out."

"The trouble is John is all right until he smokes that damn dagga."

"How do you know he smokes dagga?"

"You can see his eyes get all bloodshot and vague, and he walks around the garden like he's in a trance. He just lets the hose-pipe flood the dahlias. And sometimes you can smell it coming from his room."

It had been years since I'd been in John's room, or Emily's for that matter. Their rooms were situated against the high back wall of our property, and you had to cross our small backyard to get to them.

When I was small, Emily always shooed me out of her room. The only thing I remembered was that the room was spotlessly clean, and Isaac, Emily's husband, used to come back and sleep there on Friday and Saturday nights. Oh yes, her bed was raised off the floor on four bricks—to keep it well clear of the evil tokoloshe, she told me—and the floor itself was red and polished regularly with Sunbeam Floor Polish to make it shine . . . and shine . . . and shine.

"Let's go in the new car!" Mannie shouted from the bedroom.

"But the Greenbaums only live on Athol Drive," Mom answered. "It's a nice walk."

Mannie despised walking. I suppose lumbering his hefty frame from place to place must have been one heck of an effort.

7

My relationship with Alan was getting intense. One Sunday we all went for this picnic at Giloolie's Farm. Merv parked the van under the willows for some shade. It was very hot and dry. I don't think it had rained for months. The river there at Giloolie's was reduced to a trickle.

Still, the place was crowded out with people having their braaivleis. The air was delicious with meat smells.

Merv and Cyril started our braai while we girls unpacked the picnic. A rugby ball came flying across our tablecloth spread on the grass. Steve picked it up and booted it back to the group of sunburnt chaps who were playing on the fields.

"Come have a kick!" one of them shouted in Afrikaans, and Steve accepted their invitation. He ran off to join them.

Poor Carol! She didn't see much of Steve the whole afternoon. He played rugby with those Afrikaners the whole time, and even after Alan and I came back from the koppies, he was still playing with those guys.

I think Merv must have been coaching Alan during the week on how to handle girls, because Alan seemed determined to get me on my own somewhere.

"Anybody want to come for a walk with Ruth and me up the koppies?"

Merv and Adele said no, they'd rather stay behind in the shade, and Cyril said Rhona didn't want to climb mountains today. It all smelt a bit fishy to me as though it was prearranged and I was the only one who didn't know.

"You coming, Ruth?" Alan asked, far too keenly.

"I think there's snakes up there," I said. "I don't want to go."

But everyone chorused that there were no snakes up on the koppies, so I had to go.

We climbed for about an hour nonstop until we reached the peak of the koppies. The air was very dry and hot and everything shimmered in the heat. We walked through these wild groves of flaming protea trees, talking mostly about Alan's course.

"We had to cut up this frog on Friday," Alan said. "We had to pin its arms and legs to the board like Jesus Christ, then peel away its skin and pin that back to the board like a waistcoat. When it was lying there like an open cupboard, we had to find all its internal organs."

"Sounds luscious," I said.

"The worst part was when I had it all open with its heart cut out and its stomach everywhere, it suddenly gave this jump."

"God! Was it still alive?" I asked.

"Of course! It jerked its arms and legs until the crucifixion pins came out, and then it jumped onto the floor and hopped away. I couldn't find it, and I was just left with its heart on the chopping board."

"You're kidding me, aren't you?"

"Jeez, are you gullible, Ruth."

When we came out of the proteas we could hear drumbeats, and as we walked further along the ridge we heard singing.

"If you walk along this ridge for a couple of miles, you'll reach Linksfield Ridge."

"Really? Is this the same koppie?"

"Of course. Don't you see Orange Grove down there?"

The houses stretched below us like Baco building sets, each neat little house with its neat little garden and many with their neat kidney-bean-shaped swimming pools. Once it had been pointed out, I recognized the crisscrossing streets of the northern suburbs.

"Look, they're doing witchcraft," Alan said, pointing to these dome-shaped twig huts up ahead. Several African women were dancing about outside the huts, dressed in their royal-blue skirts and white blouses. A man also kept rhythm with his cross made of one long branch and one short branch.

We couldn't see inside the huts, but they must have been crowded with singers. Of course, we couldn't understand any of the words, because neither of us spoke Zulu or Sotho or whatever language they were singing in. Every so often the women would also ululate—make these high-pitched warbling wails.

"That's not witchcraft," I said. "That's a Christian church, isn't it?"

"It's one of the Churches of Zion," Alan said. "They come up here every Sunday."

A rumpus broke out at one of the huts, with women ululating as if to frighten the devil himself. A group of three women came tearing out of the hut, trying to support this one immensely fat woman, whose eyes were rolling around as if she were having a fit.

"She's being possessed by her ancestors," Alan said, as if he were familiar with the rituals.

The possessed woman held her arms up toward the sky, and her fingers were jerking and spasming like they didn't belong to her. Then she collapsed in a heap on the ground, and her three companions quieted down and sat beside her.

"Come on, let's move."

As we turned to go, the bloke with the tall cross made of branches caught sight of us. He waved his cross vigorously up and down, but whether he was angry or not I couldn't tell.

Still, we beat a hasty retreat through the proteas and kept going until we found this large ledge of rocks.

"Let's stay here awhile," Alan suggested.

"Uh-uh!" I thought to myself. "Better beware! He's going to try it on now."

Alan removed his shirt and lay back in the sun.

"You can also sunbathe if you want to," he said with a smile. "Take your top off if you want to."

"No thanks," I said.

"What do you think of Rhona?" he asked me. The workings of his mind were as subtle as a brick—just removing a shirt made him think instantly of Rhona.

"She's OK," I muttered.

"What d'you mean OK?" Alan said. "She's really grob. Just a tart."

"I bet you'd rather be here with her now, than with me," I said.

"Who's kidding now, man?" he said. "I'd much rather be here with you. I can't talk two words to that cow, she's so stupid. She's only good for one thing probably, not that I'd know, of course."

"So, doesn't Cyril like intelligent girls?" I asked.

"I can't figure his taste at all," Alan said.

Alan looked up at the small white clouds drifting across the sky.

"Do you ever get the feeling that you're the only person in the universe?" he asked me.

"What do you mean? What about everyone else?"

"Everyone else is just part of the dream you're having."

"I know what you mean about a dream," I said. "I sometimes wonder if it's all a dream, and one day I will wake up and find out that I'm not Ruth but someone else who's been dreaming me."

Alan turned toward me and looked straight into my eyes.

"That's what I like about you, Ruth. I can really talk to

you." He smiled and added, "Even if you're only a part of my dream."

After chatting a bit more, I decided to go and lie on my back near him. We lay in the hot-hot sun, until we were baked to a frazzle, and the lizards thought we were good company.

Then Alan turned over and half lay over me and gave me these tender kisses. I felt so lethargic from the sun, I just let his mouth make contact with mine, and we lay there enjoying each other's touch.

He didn't try anything else, but actually there was a part of me that wanted to find out more. I would never have admitted it to Alan, but I really did like him a lot.

"Let's go before those witch doctors send the tokoloshe after us," Alan said.

"What actually is a tokoloshe, do you know?" I asked Alan. "It's some kind of spoek, isn't it?"

"It's a kind of zombie," Alan explained. "Some kind of mentally controlled dwarf-thing that the witch doctor uses to do his dirty work."

"Let's go back," I said.

Of course, Steve was still jawling with the Afrikaner boys, and Carol was in a huff.

"He's played with them all afternoon. I'm not going out with him again," she said.

"That's what you said last time," I reminded her.

"Yes, but he is good-looking, isn't he?"

"Yes, but he is so self-centered it's unreal," I said.

Cyril also looked a bit peeved. He'd caught too much sun for one thing, and his freckles were showing up like confetti on his neck and arms and under his eyes. The top of Rhona's watermelons had also caught too much sun, and she lay back in the van like a sick cow, moping every time anyone touched her sunburn.

8

The next morning I went into the kitchen to brush my teeth. I'd been doing it for about a week.

"Why you always brush your teeth in the kitchen?" Emily asked me. "This is my kitchen," she added, indignantly.

"Emily, I have to. The master is always in that bath when I have to wash. I can't stand it anymore."

"Yes, that master, he thinks of himself too much," Emily said.

It was obvious to me that she and John despised Mannie as much as I did.

"Did you dream last night, Rootie?" Emily asked, when I'd finished rinsing out my mouth in the sink.

"Yes. About this black sky with bright stars in it, and then these stars turned into white doves. I was walking on this road, and there were all these white doves around me."

"Hau! Is it Sky or is it Feathers? I will put twenty cents on Feathers, number 31."

I don't think Emily had much chance of winning that day because I hadn't told her the truth about what I had dreamt.

There was not a single bird in my dream!

Yes, there were white things flying in a black sky all right, but not one of them had feathers.

You know what they were?

They were all bras!

Playtex, the bra that fits! With Wonderlastic Spandex, the new elastic material that didn't lose its shape. Thousands of them, white as angels, floating against a black sky.

I woke up from that dream in a mad sweat.

Maybe it doesn't sound like much of a nightmare, but that was my worst dream. It made me terribly panicky to think that I was so abnormal.

The size of my breasts, or rather their lack of size, was a thing that obsessed me day and night. I don't think there was ever a moment when I forgot about it completely. Even when I was most enjoying myself, then it would come to mind like a monster from the deep and spoil everything.

I mean, I had breasts, but not the size that any healthy boy would appreciate. Luckily, so far I'd managed to avoid all inquiring hands and redirect them back to their owners.

But I guess my relationship with Alan was getting too serious. Soon he would take Merv's advice and try to find out what I was made of. If Merv got a shock when his hand went under that Joyce's bra, what would happen when Alan found out that my shape was all padding? He'd probably pass out or something.

I found these bras at John Orr's—they weren't Playtex with Wonderlastic Spandex, nor Maidenform with Tric-O-Lastic-Lace. They were just plain bras with slits in them for pads. I called them pads, but boys called them falsies. It was always a horrible word in my dictionary and made my flesh creep, but I suppose anyone who wore them was false. But what choice did I have, tell me?

At school I had kept up this falseness for so long. I took special care whenever we changed into our PT togs that no one saw my upper half. It was a strain trying to keep up pretenses forever.

Even Merle, my best friend, didn't know the half of my problems. I remember when I was in Form 1 and Maxine Orlin started developing. Boy, did I envy her! My little things were like cherries, and there she was, prettiest face in the class, and now prettiest boobs too! It made me wild with envy. I never told anybody, but it was me who sent that poison letter to her. It said: "To Maxine, I think you're an ugly witch." Of course, everyone thought Jill Suzman sent it, because Jill couldn't stand Maxine. But it was me.

And one morning, Merle had come to call for me to go to school. I called out "Coming!" from my room because I was busy changing. But she didn't wait or knock. She just came barging in. It was so awful, I picked up the first thing in sight, which was a tennis racquet, and I hit her over the head with it. Honestly, I did! It was always such a sore point with me, and I was in such a tight corner. Why she ever made friends with me again, I'll never know, but it shows what a good friend she was.

I told Mom about my problems once when I was fourteen, and she sent me to Dr. Glass. But all he said was "You're perfectly normal, nothing to worry about." Of course, it was easy for him to say—men don't have that particular problem. But when I was nearly sixteen and they still hadn't grown bigger, I began to get very neurotic about it.

I even read this letter in *Personality* where a lady recommended using paraffin. So I sneaked some paraffin into my bedroom. Three times a day I rubbed it in, but nothing happened, except I started to pong a bit.

Sometimes I lay there in my bedroom, crying just like Mom. It really bothered me that I'd grow up like her—crying all the time, I mean. She never had a problem with her bust. Hers was perfectly normal: size 36C.

I used to lie there on my bed in the dark with the venetian blinds shut, lying on my mauve bedspread matching the mauve wallpaper put up by John, of course. You could tell it was put up by him because none of the joins matched. I don't think he ever noticed that wallpaper is patterned and that the patterns are supposed to match. You could also tell that it was John who put up the venetian blinds in my room, because the bottom right corner had this fault for about six inches where the blind couldn't close. There was always a spot of daylight shining through that fault, even if you shut those blinds as tight as possible.

The problem of my small breasts really depressed me.

I used to lie there and imagine that when God was handing out gifts to people just about to be born, when he came to handing out breasts, he just passed me by. It was obvious to me that because of my problem I would never be able to go steady with anyone.

I'd probably never even get married!

And it was such a pity, because I liked Alan a lot.

PART THREE

1

LENORE KNOCKED ON MY DOOR.

"Phone for you, Ruth!"

"Who is it?"

"Surprise."

I hate it when people don't say who's on the phone.

It was Cyril, of all people.

"Ruth, would you like to come to the ballet with me on Saturday night? They're doing *Swan Lake* at the Civic."

"Wait a minute, Cyril, let me think."

The trouble was Cyril knew that Alan and I were almost going steady.

"Please, Ruth, I would really appreciate it if you came with me. It's very important to me."

"Why?" I asked.

"I can't actually say. Just believe me."

"But you know that Alan and I . . ."

"But you're not going steady with him, are you? You can give me a chance."

It was true, I wasn't going steady. So I agreed. At least it was one way of slowing things down a bit with Alan.

Cyril was immaculately dressed as usual. He had these snazzy shoes on that laced at an angle down toward the side of his feet.

"Where do you buy something like that?" I asked admiringly.

"From Italia Shoe Shop. I buy all my shoes there."

The ballet was beautiful. At least the cygnets performed their dance in time with one another, for a change.

Afterward, Cyril took me to Nitebeat, where we had these creamy cappuccinos. They've got this one red wall that is reserved for signatures of famous customers, and Cyril pointed out the names of Phyllis Spira and Gary Burne, the two dancers we'd seen earlier that evening.

"Don't you think Gary Burne is good-looking?" Cyril asked me.

"Yes, he is," I said. "What was so important about taking me out tonight?"

"I'll tell you later," he said.

Later meant up on Linksfield Ridge. We sat there looking over the northern suburbs, and he eventually got round to kissing me. I must say I felt a bit guilty about abandoning Alan, but Cyril was very passionate, and experienced. I'm sure spending time with Rhona must have taught him no end of things, but if he thought he was going to compare me to Rhona's watermelon feast, he was sadly mistaken.

Actually, I was mistaken. He didn't try to get at me. He just spoke to me very seriously.

"Do you think I'm repulsive?" he asked.

He was anything but repulsive; he was just so refined, as I've said before.

"What makes you think that?"

"Rhona said some terrible things about me," he said.

"What did Rhona say?"

"You don't find me ridiculous then?"

"Of course not," I answered.

He kissed me again really passionately.

"Thank you, Ruth," he said.

"You don't have to thank me for kissing you," I said.

"No, I just mean thank you for making me feel good. Rhona won't go out with me anymore."

"She's just a Joburg kugel," I said. "Alan calls her a first-prize cow."

"Do you think you and Alan will stay together? I mean, have I got a chance, or should I just go jump in the lake?"

2

Because Mannie had refused to go to Aunt Bertha's wedding anniversary, things were at a pretty low ebb at home. Mom only spoke to Mannie when she had to, and he looked like Charles Atlas, carrying this big injustice on his shoulders.

They still went to their bridge evening at the Greenbaums, but how they managed to play together as partners is beyond me—unless they used cigarette-smoke signals to communicate.

Mannie owned a racehorse that was stabled somewhere near Turffontein racecourse, and whenever it was in a race, his partner Ullman used to come round to collect him.

Ullman was a strange man: shorter than me, which made him about five foot three, with long white sideburns, a bald head, and a double chin. His top row of teeth were worn away—at least that's what I think they were, as I never asked him—and all you could see when he opened his mouth was this row of tooth stumps. And what came out of his mouth was often a lot worse.

"None of us should have any servants," he told Mannie one Saturday.

I thought, that's a very moral attitude for old Ullman. Until I heard what he went on to say.

"It's too dangerous! You know how white South Africa is going to end? When all the servant girls put poison in the breakfasts of the white families they work for. For sure it will be organized by the communists. They will supply the poison—it doesn't take a lot of poison to get rid of a white family—and the servants will put it in the milk or something."

Mannie didn't agree. He couldn't see anything beyond his constant need for servants.

Ullman went in for the horses in a big way.

"So Mannie, you think Kubla Khan will do better than last week?" Ullman said, as he waited for Mannie in the lounge.

"He can't do worse, that's a consolation," Mannie answered from the bedroom, where he was spooning the Brylcreem onto his locks. Kubla Khan had never come in anywhere but last.

"And how's Ruthkele?" Ullman said to me as I passed through the lounge.

"OK, thanks."

Ullman lived on the same road as us, but at the other end. He was Rita's father, and Rita and I were in the same class, though not friends. When we were younger I visited her house a few times, and she came over to mine. But we didn't get on. She was very argumentative, with strong opinions about everything. Just like her mother, who had a heavy Israeli accent with gargling "r"s, which I had to hear every time she called me Rrruth. Rita also took after her father in one respect, her appearance, which was most unfortunate for her, in my opinion.

"Mannie, hurry up!" Ullman shouted out. "By the time you're ready, they'll have crossed the finishing post."

Mannie emerged looking as spruce as possible, his blazer buttons straining under the enormous pressure of his gut. He was over six feet in height, and probably the same around his waist, I wouldn't be surprised. But it was the little man who grabbed him by the elbow and led him out of the house.

As they strolled down the path, they looked for all the world like a Jewish version of Laurel and Hardy.

"Hey, Jim, when will it rain?" Ullman asked John, who was squatting as he weeded the new dahlia patch. Mom loved dahlias, and she'd asked John to make a whole new bed of them to cover the kinky wall where Mr. Pietersen's bricklayer had botched the repair job.

"Au, Master! It is not going to rain!" John replied. He never reacted to Ullman calling him "Jim." He was used to it. Anyway, I think Ullman called all black garden boys

"Jim." Mind you, I doubt if "John" was his real name either.

"At my place," Ullman said, "hose-pipe lo garden one hour per day. Is it the same here?"

Ullman always spoke half-Zulu fanagalo to John, just like the song said, so "Zulu boy will understand." But, as a matter of fact, I didn't even know if John was from Zululand.

"Yes, Master! One hour. It is no good."

"Listen, John," Mannie interrupted, "you're taking off too much time with the fah-fee."

"I don't, Master."

"He takes off hours every day. He's a runner for the Chinaman," Mannie said to Ullman, who shook his head knowingly.

"No, Master! The Chinaman has his own runners. I'm busy in the garden all day."

"You're his runner."

"No, Master! I'm only playing fah-fee."

"Listen, John, the madam pays you to work, not to spend the day gambling. This afternoon you trim off all the edges of the grass."

"The madam wants me to dig some manure in the dahlia beds, Master."

"OK, do that also. But the lawn must be trimmed before I get back."

"I did it last week, Master."

"Yes, but you must do it every week."

"But there is no rain, Master. The grass it does not grow too much."

"Listen carefully, John, to what I say. This grass needs trimming, do you understand?"

"Yes, Master! For sure, Master!"

"Otherwise you can start wondering who's going to sign your pass-book next time."

"No, Master! The job will be finished when the master gets back."

John's garden fork plunged viciously into the dry earth, his muscular arms glistening with sweat.

"Cheeky, isn't he?" Mannie said to Ullman.

Ullman laughed. "Come on, Mannie! These garden boys are all the same."

John raised his eyes as Ullman's car hummed off down Noreen Avenue. He stood there in his long white shorts and shirt, with a cone-shaped straw hat on his head and his sandals he'd made himself with leather thongs and an old car tire, and who knows what thoughts were going on under his dark brown, shiny skin.

3

That afternoon Alan came over. We sat on the swinging sofa-chair on our stoep. He was very upset.

"Why did you go out with Cyril to the ballet?" he said.

"You've got good spies," I said.

"I didn't need spies," he said. "Cyril told me himself."

"So why can't I go out with someone if I want to?"

"Because I thought we've got a good thing going between us."

"We have," I said. "But we're not going steady. I told

you, I like going out with any boy I want. And you can't stop me."

"Did you like going out with Cyril?"

"Of course I did. He's really nice."

"Did he . . . I mean did you . . . ?" Alan was obviously very worked up about my date.

"Listen, Alan. It's none of your business really what I do with who."

Poor Alan! He looked like someone hit him across the jaw.

"Don't worry, Alan. I'm not going out with him again . . . for a while, at least."

Actually, Cyril had already phoned me to make another date, but I had put him off with a few tame excuses.

Mom brought out Cokes for us and a tin of her homemade taiglach. She called Lenore out to come and have a snack. Alan tucked into the sweet biscuits, one after another, licking his fingers and lips to clean off the syrup.

"These are wonderful, Mrs. Hirsch," he said. "Nicer than the ones we have at home."

Mom looked pleased. It was the first time she allowed some pleasantness between her and Alan. I suppose she thought that if he liked taiglach he might perhaps be Jewish after all.

Lenore was dressed really snazzily, with a tight-waisted full skirt and pink kid-glove shoes on her feet. Mom asked her to turn round so she could see how the new skirt fitted. Lenore swirled around, causing her skirt to flare up.

"Stop showing off!" I said to her.

"You look lovely," Mom said to her.

Mom never said I looked lovely. It was always, "Too

much eyeliner, Ruthie!" or "Your mini's a bit short, isn't it?"

Lenore ate one taigel—with a fork, of course—before Hilton turned up.

"Where are you going?" Alan asked.

"To Hilton's cousin's place," Lenore said.

Hilton was nearly as old as Alan, but still in matric. They walked off arm in arm.

When Mom went back indoors, Alan commented that Lenore had grown up a lot in the last few months.

"She's so self-confident," I said.

"Yes, she's nice," he said.

We rocked gently on the swing-sofa. I wanted to get him off the subject of Lenore. It grated me that Lenore didn't have any problems that showed.

Toward late afternoon, Hymie, from next door, appeared in his garden with his nanny, Betty. I suppose for people who hadn't seen Hymie, it must have been a shock.

"What's wrong with him?" Alan asked.

Hymie's eyes never focused on anyone, neither on Betty nor on Mrs. Levine, his mother. He was extraordinarily handsome in his face, almost beautiful, I would say, and at times he looked dreamy and intelligent, as if he were thinking to himself. Every now and again a smile would form on his lips as if he'd thought of something hilarious, but the smile could change suddenly into an ugly, animal-like snarl. Most of the time he made strange grunting sounds, none of them recognizable as English words. Or he would whoop like a Red Indian with his hand in front of his mouth.

"He's autistic," I explained. "He lives in a world of his own."

Betty sat on the grass trying to hold Hymie's hands still, but every so often they broke loose and he was able to punch himself in the face. His own hands were his worst enemies.

Alan took the tin of taiglach across to the fence.

"Do you think he'd like a biscuit?" Alan asked.

"Thank you, Master," Betty said, leading Hymie slowly across the next-door lawn toward us.

"And one for you too," Alan said.

"Thank you, Master," Betty said, clapping her hands twice to show her appreciation.

"Your mother won't mind, will she?" Alan asked me, as an afterthought.

Hymie lifted the sticky taigel toward his mouth, licked it, sniffed it, and held it up closely to each of his eyes. He licked it again, then threw it to the ground, at the same time slamming his fist into his eyes, and not even registering the pain.

At close quarters, it was noticeable that Hymie's eyes were black and blue, from the repeated beatings he gave himself. And the bridge of his nose was scabbed in several places from previous wounds.

"Why does he do that?" Alan asked Betty.

"I don't know, Master. The doctor says it is part of the sickness."

"Does he punch himself all of the time?" Alan asked.

"Even at night, Master, we must tie his hands together so that he can sleep."

A face appeared at one of the windows next door. It was Mrs. Levine. She looked out at her son for a moment, and at us all gathered around him.

The Levines only had the one child. Perhaps the shock

of that one child was too much—Mrs. Levine never got pregnant again. She was a remote, sad lady, but who could blame her? I hardly ever saw her with Hymie. It was as if she couldn't bear to be with him.

She kept a yellow budgie in the room where she was standing that very minute. Sometimes when I'd been in their house, she would take me to that budgie and say to it "Cheeky boy Levine! Cheeky boy Levine!" and the bird would tweet out its answer, "Cheeky boy Levine! Cheeky boy Levine!" and Mrs. Levine would turn to me with a proud, pathetic smile. I think maybe she prayed that her Hymie would one day be able to say at least as much as that yellow budgie.

4

Alan's family were DI enthusiasts. DI was what they called the Drive-In Cinema. They loved going to the DI, and distance was no problem to them. They frequented the Joburg Drive-In on the Pretoria Road, the Panorama, the Stadium, the Dakota (that's the one with the old airplane at the entrance), the Baragwanath, the Topstar (on top of the mine dump), and even the Randfontein Drive-In if there was something good showing.

The first time I went with them was to the Velskoen. I'll never forget it because they were showing *King Solomon's Mines*. We went in Mr. Gerber's old Chevrolet which was a big car, but even so we were cramped because there was Mr. and Mrs. Gerber and little Sam in the front, and Donnay, Alan, and me in the back. Bobby didn't come with us, of course; he was going somewhere with his mouth organ and his guitar and a few pals. He did ask me, though, if I'd been practicing my cricket, and when was I going to come round for another game?

The Gerber family sang all the way. They sang group songs like "My eyes are dim, I cannot see, I have not brought my specs with me," and "Alouette," where you have to mention every family member by name and then cheer as each new one gets added to the list, and then there were songs the Gerbers made up themselves:

Adam was a farmer who bought a farm with Eve.
They ate too many apples and then they had to leave.
Eve bought a café and taught herself to bake,
but got in awful trouble all because of a snake.

I loved singing with them.

As we got near the Velskoen, Donnay said should she hide. I don't know if Mr. Gerber was a bit embarrassed by this, but as the cat was out of the bag, he said yes, she might as well. So she lay down at our feet, and Alan spread a blanket over our laps so that she was well and truly hidden.

Once we were in the DI she popped up again, but at least that was one less person to pay for.

The reason I'll never forget that film is because during the exciting bit an electric storm broke loose. The forked lightning was so vicious it looked like it was ripping the sky open. The fireworks show was all around us and very close: you couldn't even count to three in between the lightning flash and the thunderclap, which meant the flashes were striking less than three miles away. And then there was one flash that arrived the same time as its thunder, and we could actually see the lightning strike the drive-in screen and slither along the top of it.

After the electrics came the rain, heavy rain with huge drops so that we couldn't see the film at all, and we all cheered because we thought the drought had come to an end, but it lasted only a few minutes and then it was all over, and Stewart Granger could get on with finding King Solomon's Mines.

During the storm we were all quite frightened, and Donnay grabbed on to Alan for comfort, and he, of course, grabbed on to me. Donnay didn't know where to look first—the film, the storm, or Alan's hands going round my body. I prayed that Alan wouldn't get too agitated by the storm and start investigating certain parts of my anatomy that were camouflaged behind John Orr padding.

Even after the storm had died down, Alan must have still been frightened, because he kept holding on to me like that until we got home. So I survived another night.

5

I got home well after midnight to discover that the storm had agitated other people as well. I found Mom at the back door screaming like mad at Emily's husband, Isaac, who was so drunk he had to hold up our mulberry tree in case it toppled over.

"You go to your room, Isaac!" she was shouting.

"I must kill him first, Madam!" Isaac shouted back, pointing at John who was standing against the back wall.

"That boy is no good. Emily is my wife, Madam."

Emily was hiding in her room and wouldn't show her face. Our cocker spaniels were wagging their tails, thinking what fun it was to have attention in the middle of the night.

"We'll talk about it in the morning, Isaac, when your head is not swimming in beer."

"No, Madam, I must kill him now," Isaac said, fumbling around in the dark near the mulberry tree.

Mom and I saw the glint at the same time. Isaac was holding something long and shiny in his shaking hand—a panga knife.

I thought it would be better if Mom and I beat a hasty retreat into our house and call someone else to deal with it. Not Mannie— all six foot two of him was indoors somewhere dreaming of his Kubla Khan coming in last in the afternoon's race. He wouldn't let a small thing like a drunken jealous husband with a panga disturb his night's sleep. But maybe we could call the police. Mom obviously didn't think that was necessary.

"Isaac!" she yelled, with the same firmness of tone that any police officer would have been proud of in those circumstances. "Isaac! Come here! Come right here to these stairs!"

Isaac hobbled across the yard.

"Now give me that knife immediately!"

Isaac looked up at Mom, and for an ugly moment I thought he was going to give it to her blade first. But as the panga made its way from the one person to the other, it half changed direction, so that Mom was able to grab it sideways by the handle.

"Good!" she said. "Now, Isaac, listen to me. Emily is

waiting for you in your room. She says she has done nothing with John. Tomorrow you will talk with her when your head is clear. Now you must go to sleep, or I will call the police and tell them that you have been carrying this knife, and they will put you in jail for a few months. Do you want that?"

"No, Madam."

Mom then stepped back into our kitchen, closed the back door, and bolted it. Then she went straight to the toilet.

It was only when she had returned to the kitchen to make herself a cup of tea that I saw how pale she was. Her hands were trembling, and her eyes had sunk deep into their sockets. She suddenly looked very old to me. I hadn't noticed the wrinkles on her face before—or perhaps I had but not made a conscious note of it. And beneath her eyes you could see little bluish-red veins in the surface of her skin. Examined close up like that she didn't look well.

"You sit down, Mom; I'll make you tea."

Even though she didn't take sugar, I put a teaspoonful in her cup, to help her get over the shock.

"You were fantastic, Mom. I was so scared when Isaac pulled out that panga."

"So was I. I've never been so scared in my life."

She sipped her tea and her hands stopped trembling, but that worn look on her face never changed. In fact, from that night I always saw Mom as a much older person. I hadn't realized how much she'd aged since her marriage to Mannie.

"That John really is no good," Mom said.

"Do you think he's been interfering with Emily?"

"Oh, I don't know about that. Emily can take care of herself. But he smokes that dagga all the time, and he goes to Betty's shebeen every Thursday."

"What d'you mean?" I asked. "Which Betty?"

"You know, Betty from next door. The Levine's Betty."

"Come off it, Mom. Betty's really nice. She doesn't run a shebeen."

"Well, you're the only person in this part of the world who doesn't think so," Mom said.

"How do you know?"

"Every Thursday now for months, Mrs. Levine takes Hymie to that healing doctor in Benoni. That's when Betty runs her shebeen. Just on Thursdays. You must have seen the stream of men she gets on a Thursday."

"It's her day off, Mom. All the servants around here get lots of visitors. And she gets lots of women visitors too."

"Well, who knows what these shiksas get up to in those back rooms. Haven't you seen the way they dress? It must be a high-class brothel back there."

That was the only time I ever heard Mom use that word "brothel." But I couldn't believe that Betty was that sort of person.

"John specially takes off Thursday also so that he can go there. It's disgusting. Mrs. Levine really should do something about the situation."

"Does she know?"

"Who can say? Even if she does, she wouldn't want to lose Betty because who else would look after poor Hymie all day?"

.

6

At the beginning of the second school term, Rhona Tabatznik showed us her brain. And she showed it to us in the middle of Mrs. Joffe's class.

It was supposed to be an English class, but Mrs. Joffe had this scheme to sell books to all the pupils of the school. Her excuse was that we needed to broaden our reading experience, but I never heard her explain exactly what was wrong with bookshops or the public library. She had this cardboard box full of *Vanity Fair* and *St. Joan* and *The Thirty-Nine Steps* and other minor classics which she had to lug from one classroom to another. She used to spend half the lesson unpacking them and displaying them along the chalk ledge of the blackboard. The other half of the lesson she would spend packing them back into her cardboard box again. If there was any time to spare, she would count the money she had taken that day into little piles on the table in front of her and write the details in her little books. If there was any time to spare after that, she got us to read our set work, *Far from the Madding Crowd*. So it's no wonder with all that education, that after my matric examination I still didn't know how this place Madding got itself into the title.

It was while Mrs. Joffe was counting her money that Rhona showed us her brain. Mrs. Joffe was as broad as she was tall, which made her about the shape of a large bullfrog with a croaky voice to match. I felt sorry for her really because her neck was abnormally fat and puffy with rolls of flab that quivered when she spoke. She was actually a decent person if you got to know her, which I did, because she was the one I once asked about puberty and rate of breast growth.

She had taken me aside and spoken quite frankly to me about it. Some time later she brought me in this book about adolescent development, which had these coy diagrams of females in it. The book didn't help at all, because it said most girls developed between twelve and fifteen. I was already fifteen at the time, and the only thing that was developing was my inferiority complex.

But Mrs. Joffe was always pleasant to me after that, and she couldn't help what she looked like either. Sometimes I thought it must be even worse to have a body disfigurement like hers than just to have a severe shortage in the breast department.

While Mrs. Joffe was packing away her books, Rhona Tabatznik got out this thing from her desk. It was like a balloon, but she had filled it with water. I had never seen such a thing before, but I knew it was a Frenchie as soon as I laid eyes on it. It was repulsive. How Rhona could do that was completely beyond me. I thought that showed exactly what her brain was like—smutty and filled with nothing but dirty water.

She made it into this sausage shape and pointed it under her skirt so that all the girls could see her cleverness. Then she passed the Frenchie round to a few girls who wanted to make sure it was the real thing, and not something she got at a birthday party. I wouldn't have touched that thing in a million years, especially when I thought her brother Ezra might have had some contact with it.

Finally the excitement died down when the bell rang,

and Mrs. Joffe took up her burden to take to her next class.

In the afternoon, Rhona bunked classes and we didn't see her again. Actually, we didn't ever see her again at Fairview Girls High. That Mrs. Joffe might have looked peculiar, but there wasn't anything that went on in any class that she didn't see.

It was the following day before we heard that Rhona Tabatznik had been expelled.

7

The next time I went round to the Gerbers for a braai, the old general was missing.

"He's gone into Tara Hospital," Alan said. "We don't know if he'll ever come out of there. He's got Parkinson's very badly."

But Alan's granny wasn't showing her upset. She took me into the lounge and sang a sort of Russian folk song for me and danced a folk-dance accompaniment. She must have had that song in her memory for a long time because she told me she learned it at school. That meant she must have learned it way back at the beginning of the century. I could see where all the Gerbers had inherited their musical talents from.

Alan recorded her singing on his newly acquired Phillips reel-to-reel tape recorder. His granny shook her head in disbelief when he played it back to her.

"The machine can sing the Russian song!"

She was particularly cheerful all day, and I couldn't understand it. Perhaps no one had told her that her husband had been taken into Tara with Parkinson's.

I mentioned it later to Alan, and he said that the old lady was putting it out of her mind or, in other words, pretending. She was paranoid about illness or dying, and whenever she heard one of those words spoken she always spat twice toward the ground to ward off the evil eye.

One thing about the Gerbers, they were all into music in a big way. And when they found out I wasn't, they were determined to educate me.

"You've never heard Bob Dylan?" Bobby said to me after lunch and before the cricket game started. "You don't know what you're missing."

He took me upstairs to his room where he had a portable record player and told me to listen carefully.

He wasn't kidding about carefully. Bob Dylan sang through his nose, and I could hardly make out one word.

It was the one about the times they are a-changing. Of course it was a great song, but when I first heard it, I thought this guy should take a few singing lessons from Neil Sedaka.

Bobby's room consisted mostly of his books. And somewhere underneath them all there must have been a desk or a table and I suppose a bed. Most of the books were about politics, a subject I didn't have the slightest inclination toward.

"So, Ruth, it beats Elvis, doesn't it?"

"Yes," I said, none too convincingly.

"The whole world is changing just like Bob Dylan says, and congressmen and politicians better heed the call."

"What call is that?" I asked.

"For change. I mean, things have been really changing

in this country since the Sharpeville Massacre. The world is beginning to wake up to the atrocities going on here."

"I'm not really interested in politics," I said. "I don't know much about what's been going on."

"Really?" Bobby said. "It's your country. Don't you care?"

"I suppose so."

"Don't you think it's wrong that we white people live so well? We've got one of the highest standards of living in the whole world. But the Africans live in poverty, and they have one of the highest rates of infant mortality in the world. Their children die like flies."

"I suppose it's unfair," I said. "But what can we do about it?"

"First we must get rid of our own prejudices. Then we must try to help the situation of Africans wherever we can. And we must teach the whites that what we're doing to Africans is wrong. Every drop of protest will help in the long run."

It was interesting talking to Bobby, but still I was relieved when Alan appeared at the doorway.

"What are you doing with my girlfriend in here?" Alan asked him.

"Moenie worry nie!" Bobby said, giving me a small friendly hug. "I won't steal her from you. Even though she's much too nice for you. Anyway, what would Dawn say?"

That was the first I'd heard of Bobby's girlfriend, and I met her later the same day.

Alan obviously felt that it wouldn't be right for me to go and play cricket without seeing his room also. So he led the way and closed the door behind us.

His bedroom was a bit strange. On the floor were two impala skins, and wrapped around the side of his bed was a long snakeskin more than a foot wide.

"What snakeskin is that?" I asked.

"Python," he said. "Seventeen feet long, and there's the bullet hole where I shot it."

"God, I would have died if I came across that in the wild. Where was it?"

"You're such a potz!" he said. "You mustn't believe everything I say. I bought that in a curio shop."

"Oh," I said. "I don't know how you manage to sleep with that around the bed."

"I like it," Alan said. "In African belief the python is divine. He is the Great Serpent whose seven thousand coils brought the universe into being."

On his desk lay thick textbooks with zoological drawings.

"We cut up a dogfish this week," he said. "It was putrid. The smell alone nearly made me give up medicine on the spot. It wasn't like the frog we cut up last time—this thing had been pickled. I had to leave the lab and go out for some fresh air."

"Shame," I said.

I thought he was going to do a bit more studying of zoology when he put his arm around me and pulled me in close for a kiss, but his father yelled out that the cricket test match was being sadly delayed on account of us.

Steve had arrived with not only his lucky cap, but also his cricketing whites. He was showing little Sam how to stroke the ball with the cricket bat.

"No tantrums today," Mr. Gerber said with a big smile,

but I didn't know if he was saying it to little Sam or to Steve.

Dawn didn't play cricket. She was a quiet person, with long, straight blond hair and gentle brown eyes. She sat talking with Mrs. Gerber and Alan's grandmother throughout our game.

My play had improved since the time before. Instead of scoring just three runs, I scored four. Mind you, they also gave me four innings instead of three.

Little Sam didn't emigrate to any foreign places, and Steve scored sixty-two runs not out and didn't want the game to stop for tea.

"I've got the feel of this wicket now," he said. "Can't we have tea a bit later?"

"Listen, Steve," Mr. Gerber said, "even the England cricket team stops for tea."

So we stopped for tea, and little Sam put a piece of Mrs. Gerber's world-famous custard cake down on this deck chair just as Steve was going to sit on it. It was a waste of a good piece of custard cake, and the stains on Steve's white shorts seriously upset his feel of the wicket, because he was out first ball after play resumed.

8

Prejudice is a strange thing. Mostly you don't know if you've got it or not, and if you think you have, then you probably haven't. But if you think you haven't, then most likely you do have it!

Basically I thought I was charitable to blacks and all that. At school I was involved in a project to collect half-used exercise books which would then be sent to the schools in the townships for the kids to write in. Our teacher had brought in a few of their exercise books to show us how valuable paper was to those black students. I'm telling you, they wrote so small you could hardly read it, and they crushed their writing into every square inch of the page.

There was also the time a few years back when Mannie was courting Mom and pretending to be cultured and interested in films. We came out of the His Majesty's and saw that piccanin playing kwela music on his penny whistle. My God, he looked so cold! He was barefoot and only wore broken shorts and a broken T-shirt. And he was dancing to keep warm. Nonstop dancing to keep warm. I felt so sorry for him. Mom and Mannie walked on ahead toward where our car was parked, but I lingered behind and couldn't take my eyes off the boy. In the end I took off the woolen cardigan I was wearing—it was a special embroidered one that my mom had bought for me—and I went up to the boy and said, "Here! It's for you because you play such nice music." The boy stopped his kwela music for a minute to put it on. He didn't care that it was a girl's cardigan, and he smiled at me before blowing his penny whistle once more.

Mom was mad at me, you can imagine. She said, how can you give away a cardigan to every poor beggar you meet? That wasn't how I looked at it—I just saw one cold boy.

To me, people are people, aren't they?

And prejudice is prejudice.

9

One evening we were in Merv's dad's van, cruising through Hillbrow. There was Alan and me, and Steve and his new girlfriend Sharon in the back, and Merv and Adele, as usual, in the front. Cyril was not with us because he said he had some dentistry project to work on.

I watched the front of Sharon's shirt as we bumped along. I couldn't help it. I always did this with girls I met for the first time until I could gauge what size they were.

I had to stop staring when Sharon nearly caught my eye. It always happened like that. I'm sure girls must have thought I was perverted looking at them so closely in that particular area.

As usual, she was bigger than me.

We stopped at Fontana for these foot-long hot dogs, which really were about a foot long. We ate them on the pavement watching the world go by. Merv was pretty gross with his male humor, but Steve laughed along like he was an adolescent, which he probably was inside that skinny body of his. Anyhow, he'd had too much Gordon's Dry Gin to tell a joke from a tragedy.

"Do you want a bite of my foot-long?" Merv asked Adele, while Steve giggled to himself.

She was not at all amused and kept her face dead straight, biting into her own foot-long with as much delicacy as she could manage, considering that mayonnaise and tomato sauce were oozing out between the two rolls.

"Yours is nowhere near a foot long!" Steve gurgled.

"You know what happened with old Prof Gottlieb last lecture?" Merv asked the girls. "Should I tell them, Steve?"

Steve, naturally, encouraged Merv's titillations.

"He's our zoology prof," Merv explained, "and he was talking about this tribe in the Amazon who are supposed to have the longest penises in the world. I honestly don't know if he was charfing around or not."

"Of course he wasn't," Steve said, though all he probably knew about Amazon tribes was that they lived near the Amazon.

Adele stopped eating her foot-long and looked as though she might squash it in Merv's face if he continued. It's funny with Adele—she didn't seem to like Merv's lavatory humor at all, but she held on to him like he was the best catch that ever came out of the sea.

"What Prof Gottlieb said must have offended one or two of the female students," Merv said.

"I'm not surprised," Adele said.

"This girl Lorraine Johnson got up while he was talking, and she marched out the room. I heard her say 'Disgusting!' as she went past me."

"I would have too," Adele said.

"But you know what Prof Gottlieb said? He said: 'Miss Johnson, there's no need to hurry! The next plane for the Amazon doesn't leave Jan Smuts till six-thirty!'"

Merv and Steve rolled around with laughter, choking on their foot-longs.

"Lorraine will never be able to come to Gottlieb's lectures again," Merv said. "He made such a fool of her."

Adele was annoyed with Merv after he told that story. For at least three minutes she was extremely annoyed.

Then he whispered something in her ear, and she immediately displayed her astonishing powers of forgiveness, and she was all smiles again. One thing for sure, if that was my boyfriend I would have told him exactly where to step off.

We spent the night in this basement dive called the Tadpole, listening to these jazz musicians. They were fantastic, especially the pianist, who wore dark glasses and a peaked cap. I thought Steve might get on well with him because of sharing this interest in peaked caps, but Steve was restless the whole night. He kept saying he hated jazz and wouldn't drink the strong coffee we ordered for him. We all drank ours because that's what you do in a jazz club, but Steve didn't care what you do in a jazz club, and he poured what remained of his Gordon's Dry into an empty cup and swigged that all night. By the end of the evening, he forgot he was listening to jazz, or any other kind of music for that matter, and he slept with his head on the tabletop. It was lucky Sharon enjoyed the music, because she couldn't have enjoyed Steve's company.

When we emerged like moles from that den, Hillbrow was busy as anything because it was getting on for midnight.

As we were walking back to the van, we saw this bloke who looked very much like Cyril, with an Ipana smile, the only difference being that this bloke was wearing dark glasses. He was either another jazz pianist or he wanted to avoid the glare of the neons. But what nearly convinced me that it was in fact Cyril were his snazzy shoes, laced up diagonally and gleaming as he spoke to this African woman.

He looked like he was asking for directions, which was surprising if it was Cyril, because I knew he was perfectly well acquainted with the area and wasn't likely to be lost. Also I wasn't quite sure why he would ask directions of an African woman who looked to me like she was a street-walker. I mean she was one of those women with high high-heels, miniskirt, low-cut blouse, and a black European wig. And, of course, her face had pale blotches from being lightened with Ambi Special, the best skin-lightener in the world—eighty-seven cents per large tube.

This lady was pointing to the top floor of a block of flats, and I thought, why would he be asking directions to the servants' quarters of that block of flats?

Merv must have also been thinking these things because he called out "Cyril!"

The bloke with the dark glasses and Italia shoes turned suddenly and walked off, so I don't suppose he wanted his name shouted all over Hillbrow. But how Cyril could pretend that we hadn't seen him was beyond me. He could have at least waved hello to us or something.

As Cyril disappeared toward the block of flats, Merv said: "So that's his dental project, hey? The teeth of African prostitutes."

10

People were saying it was one of the worst droughts for many a year. Farm dams were dry; river spruits were reduced to a trickle; the northern part of the Transvaal known as the "Belt of Sorrow" hadn't had a single drop of rain for over a year; there was talk of the Vaaldam reaching a dangerously low level; water was rationed on the Rand; and finally, hose-pipe watering in the northern suburbs was banned altogether.

Some of the lush gardens even began to dry out; the lawns yellowed in parts and gave off a dust as you walked on them. John struggled desperately to save our lawn, using a bucket that he filled by the tap, but it was a losing battle.

And he couldn't stop, either, when he injured his arms. I wasn't sure what had happened to him, but there he was one day with a white bandage on each forearm.

He wouldn't say anything when I asked him what had happened, so I asked Emily, who only told me that he had cut himself badly on each arm. She seemed reluctant to talk about it.

After he took off the bandages there were bad scabs, and it took weeks for them to heal. It must have been painful carrying heavy buckets of water with those wounds, but he tried to defeat the drought, and every day he'd water the lawn.

People in high places, like the leading churchmen and the brother of the minister of justice, had secret, inside information from on high about the cause of the drought. According to them, the offending item was, believe it or not, the miniskirt! Moral decline among the people dried up the rain—that's according to the Bible, they said. It was the first I'd ever heard that women wore miniskirts in the Bible days.

And it wasn't just the miniskirt that was under suspicion for causing the drought—what about the Pill? If the mini-

skirt caused drought, the Pill would probably cause earth-
quakes, unless the people woke up to the iniquity of their
ways pretty soon.

11

Ullman was at our house one day hanging about uselessly,
waiting for Mannie to get home from somewhere or other,
and I needed to get to extra Latin lessons I was having up
in Sydenham.

I usually went by bus and foot, but seeing me leave, Ullman offered me a lift. I was thankful—he hadn't ever done
much for me before, that's for sure. I climbed into his
Mercedes and we were off.

But wait a minute! This wasn't toward Sydenham—this
was Sandringham we were passing through.

"I just want to go somewhere first, won't take a minute," he said.

But by the time I saw Edenvale Hospital I began to have
serious doubts about what was going on. The way he was
taking the curves at high speed, maybe he was thinking of
crossing the border into Mozambique.

"How much further?" I asked.

"Around this corner."

Well, around that corner was nothing more than a de-
serted gravel road on a hill, as far as I could see, with
nothing but parched veld all around.

"Lovely place," he said.

I looked around to see what was lovely about it. There
were a few pondokkies miles away on the other side of the

valley, but they weren't anything special to look at.

Then I realized that Ullman thought it was lovely because there was no one else about to see how lovely it was, except for him and me.

This realization was accompanied by the shock-horror of my life! The bastard's chubby hands grabbed my breasts firmly as he swung round over me and placed his lips over mine.

It was unbelievably revolting!

I started to struggle out of his grasp, and I spat in his face, and I screamed hysterically.

"You bastard! You dirty bastard!"

I punched my fists against his face repeatedly, and I tried to open the car door. But he had an iron grip on me and wouldn't let go.

"You bastard! Let go!"

I kicked and punched and screamed ceaselessly, until suddenly he pulled back and sat bolt upright on his side of the car, as if he were waking out of a dream.

"I'm sorry!" he said. "I'm sorry! I don't know what I was doing."

I was white-hot with anger and terror. I struggled to open the door.

"I'm sorry," he kept saying over and over again. "I thought you wanted it."

I jumped out the car and started running back along the road the way we'd come.

What did the bastard say? How could he think I wanted it? Sis, he was so ugly and old and revolting. And such a bastard! He was only thinking of himself.

Ullman must have sat in the car for a few moments deciding what to do. He would never have been able to catch me up running, so he started the car and turned it round to come after me.

I ran as if the devil were chasing me, and maybe he was! I couldn't reach the main road before the Mercedes would catch me up, so I ran out across the field in a diagonal direction toward some trees.

PART FOUR

1

I SAT IN A STRANGE KITCHEN, DRINKING
Lecol orange squash and nibbling Eet-sum-mor short-
bread.

The servant girl was phoning the madam to come home
quickly.

I was still out of breath and in a state of shock.

I never expected the first male ever to touch my breasts
would be that old bastard with his row of stump teeth, the
father of a friend of mine, and husband of a woman I actually knew.

Thank God I'd reached the row of houses backing onto
the fields.

"The madam is coming," the nanny said. "Are you better now?"

I asked to use the bathroom.

In the mirror I saw this unknown person.

There was a girl looking much older than sixteen with mascara running down her cheeks, thick smudged eyeliner, and hair teased up into a fashionable but disheveled beehive, with a fringe down to her eyebrows. Her lips were stained brightly with coral lipstick.

Lower down in the mirror I could see her full bust, puffed out with its John Orr padding. And from her tight-fitting miniskirt, her tanned thighs protruded.

That girl looked like one heck of a cheap tart!

Was that the girl Ullman had seen?

2

When I got home, I rushed into Mom's arms.

She was hysterical when she heard what had happened.

"Oy gevalt!" she sobbed repeatedly. "Oy vay, Ruthie! At least you're untouched, thank God. That Ullman's a piece of rubbish. Why did you ever take a lift with that pig?"

She went storming into Mannie's bedroom.

"You know what your bladdy partner's done to my Ruthie?"

They screamed at each other for half an hour.

"Of course I'm going to charge him with assault!" Mom said. "What do you think? I'll speak to Zlotkin first thing in the morning. You think that pig's going to get away with it?"

"Take it easy! Calm down!" Mannie said. "What did he do? He didn't hurt her. He didn't rape her. He tried to kiss her, that's all."

"What do you mean that's all? Ruth is sixteen. She's a child. And he's got a wife. Sis! He's degenerate."

"What do you know?" Mannie shouted. "He's divorcing his wife."

"Since when?" Mom said. "And what's that got to do with it anyway? Are you defending him? He's a father of a girl Ruth's age. He is going to pay for this. I'll smear his name all over the newspapers."

"Stop screaming! You'll burst a blood vessel! If you ruin him, you'll ruin me! Can't you see that? It will destroy my business."

"Is that all you think of? You're no better than he is! Get yourself a new partner! That man is the dregs of the earth."

3

For two days they didn't speak to each other.

Then it all came out in a flood of bad feeling. They screamed their points of view at each other. And when they weren't screaming, they boiled with indignation.

After a week they reached a compromise that Ullman would never again set foot in our house, nor would his name ever be mentioned.

But he was still Mannie's partner, and he still lived down our road, driving his Mercedes past our house as if nothing had happened.

I couldn't stand living in that house anymore. Not with Mannie there. He reminded me of Ullman, and it made me sick. In fact, I was disgusted with the whole male species.

And some females too, like Lenore, who was getting on my nerves.

I decided to stop walking to school with her. She never walked home with me, anyway. She waited for Hilton to pick her up after school every day. So it wasn't much of a decision to stop walking with her in the mornings. She asked for it. She was the one who brought up how I looked.

"It doesn't suit you, Ruth, believe me."

"Why do you interfere in the way I dress?"

"Because you're my sister, and I hear what people say about you."

"Oh, what do they say?"

"I can't tell you."

"Is it so terrible?"

"I can't say."

"Come on, Lenore, you know you were going to tell me anyway."

"They say it doesn't suit you."

"Is that all?"

"And that you're trying too hard to make yourself attractive."

"Shut up, Lenore! Who cares what other people think? What do they know?"

"Well, you asked me to tell you. Don't get cross with me."

"I'm not cross with you!"

That was the last time we walked to school together. After that, Hilton accompanied her in the mornings as well.

I waited for Mom to get rid of Mannie. I gave her a clear ultimatum—him or me—but she didn't reply.

And I waited for Mom to get Zlotkin to charge Ullman with assault, but she never did. Perhaps because I wasn't hurt. But she didn't know what it felt like inside me.

I felt so humiliated, so dirty. I wanted to wash myself clean of all that had happened, but how? My own family was useless to me: instead of giving me support, I had the distinct feeling they half blamed me for what had happened. It was impossible. I had to do something before I burst.

Ten days after the incident, I packed my suitcase again and went to stay at Barney and Helen's.

4

Alan kept in touch with me. Of course, I never told him what had happened with Ullman. As far as he knew I'd left home because of my stepfather.

It was a harrowing time. I was constantly upset, and Mom couldn't bear my being away from her. She came to see me every evening and tried to persuade me to return home. But I was adamant that I would never go back, not while *he* was there. If Mom chucked out Mannie, then I'd go back like a shot. But until then, never!

Alan tried his best to cheer me up. He got me involved in building a float for the Rag Day procession on the grounds of this Houghton house. Dozens of medics pasted tons of papier-mâché on to what was supposed to be the moon, but something must have gone wrong in the planning. Personally, if you would have asked me, I'd have said that it wasn't a good idea to mix so much Lion Beer in the papier-mâché mixture. It didn't harden properly on the wood and chicken-wire frame, so the moon looked as if it would collapse as soon as man stepped on it for the first time. In any event, I don't think those medics were the best float-builders in the history of the university. Also, the connection between moon-men and medicine seemed very obscure to me.

I was given the task of tearing paper into strips, and by the time midnight came, I must have torn enough paper to reach from Houghton to the moon, via Naboomspruit. Still, it took my mind off my own problems, and it was great fun, especially as I wasn't even a university student yet.

5

I lasted a week at my uncle and aunt's place. Then Uncle Barney sat me down for a chat. He told me how pleasant it was for him and Helen to have me stay at their house, and how he sympathized with me because of Mannie and all the rest of it, but to come to the point, he was very worried about Mom.

"You must be able to see it, Ruth. She's going to have a nervous breakdown if she goes on like this. Really she needs a break from her work and from Mannie. But she doesn't listen to anyone's advice. She's just worried about you."

"But I'm OK," I said. "I like it here."

"I know you do, but you have to see it from your mom's point of view as well. She feels like she's let you down, and she's beating herself over the head with remorse."

"What can I do about it?" I asked. "She's pathetic."

"Pathetic she may be, Ruth, but she needs your love desperately."

The next day Mom fetched me home.

6

The night before Rag Day, we were all standing outside the Metro Cinema on Jeppe Street. There was Merv and Alan and me and a few others, and a whole queue of people waiting to be let in to see *The Sound of Music*.

We were all chatting away when suddenly who should appear but Steve. And he's screaming in public. I thought, my God, he must be heavily under the influence of Gordon's Dry to be screaming like that.

"Merv, you bastard!" he shouts out, and every soul in that queue turned round to see what was going on. I could have died of embarrassment.

"What's up?" Merv asks.

"You've been sleeping with my girlfriend, that's what's up!" Steve screams, and he looks like he's off his head with jealousy.

I couldn't work out which girlfriend he meant, because he went through them so quickly. Also I couldn't work out why he was so bothered, because he didn't seem to care so much for any of his girlfriends. And anyway, Merv was so loyal to Adele.

"She's my girl," he screams out. "And that's the last time you're ever going to betray me!"

Steve was getting so melodramatic, I couldn't believe

it. Nor could I believe what happened next.

He pulled out a revolver!

And he aimed the revolver and pointed it straight at Merv!

"Don't shoot!" Merv shouts out. "It's all a mistake."

But before anyone could stop Steve, a shot rang out. Merv collapsed to the ground, and this red blood oozed out from his chest. Adele knelt pathetically over him.

The crowd from the Metro gathered round and wanted to lynch Steve there and then, but at that moment, by some coincidence, these four blokes came walking round the corner carrying a coffin.

Everybody picked up Merv and dropped him in the coffin. And then I saw that along the side of the coffin was written "Support Rag Day tomorrow!"

The whole thing was a stunt! I couldn't believe it. Alan could at least have told me.

"We only told Adele," he explained, "because we didn't want her to die of a heart attack. Did the squirting tomato sauce really fool you?"

I didn't want to be a bad sport—after all, the money from Rag Day went to charity. So I tried to calm my palpitating heart as we carried the coffin down to Bree Street.

Later that evening we all did another stunt. We rolled this huge roll of toilet paper—it was huge, five or six feet in diameter—right down Commissioner Street. Or should I rather say, we unrolled it down Commissioner Street. People couldn't believe their eyes.

On Rag Day I walked alongside the "First Medic on the Moon" float, collecting money in these tins. I was dressed as a Martian, painted green, though I hadn't realized that my green would run as soon as I started sweating. Alan and Merv were two of the blokes in spaceman outfits walking on the moon, which was still tacky from being painted a few hours before. Together with dozens of other students, we had stayed up all night working on it to get it finished in time.

By the end of the procession, I was able to witness for myself the connection between medicine and the moon, because more than half of the blokes in space helmets seemed to be overcome with dizziness and required resuscitation from the nurses, while the other half needed attention when the moon collapsed, just near Harrison Street. It's lucky there were so many nurses on that float to lend a hand, although I suppose they were quite hampered in their first-aid work by their stockings and suspenders getting caught up in their stethoscopes.

At the Rag Ball, the spaceman and his Martian girlfriend had a cosmic time. We were exhausted from staying up the night before and from walking halfway across Joburg and then back again, but we danced the twist and the locomotion and the cha-cha and the lebamba and the samba and the rumba, not to mention a few waltzes and quicksteps and rock and roll, all without flaking out. Finally, in the back of the van on the way home, we sagged against each other in an exhausted state of contentment.

7

Little Hymie from next door was made to wear a red crash helmet.

"The madam says he must wear it all day," Betty explained, "because now he bangs his head on the wall."

"Shame," I said. "Can't the doctor give him something to stop him hurting himself?"

"He takes plenty tablets, but they are no good."

As we spoke, Hymie attempted to punch himself in the face. Betty tried to restrain his vicious little fists.

Betty was so patient with Hymie. It struck me that no mother could have done a better job. And it left Mrs. Levine free to teach her yellow-feathered Cheeky Boy new words. Betty always had a smile for her Hymie. She cuddled him so close to her body all day, like she was protecting him from something. She really loved that child, that's for sure.

But how could the same woman that I saw before me also run a shebeen in her back room? I knew we didn't know much about what the servants were getting up to, but it was confusing to me to think that Betty could be immoral.

Ever since Mom had mentioned the shebeen next door, I had been on the lookout to see if it could possibly be true. One thing was for sure, Betty had a lot of visitors on a Thursday. At two o'clock after school I would see them going in one by one round the back. And on my word of honor, it's true, I even saw John going in by their back door. And he wasn't wearing his long shorts and native sandals either. Oh no! He was dressed in European clothes—long trousers, two-tone shoes, a pink shirt, and a checked sports jacket. I waited for him to come out. He was in there twenty-five minutes and he emerged jiving and clicking his fingers like he was the Number One Joburg Jawler, and he was still jiving and clicking when he passed out of sight where Noreen Avenue bends.

There were no end of customers at Betty's establishment. Sometimes, an overspill would develop on the pavement, and once, even, a portable gramophone blared out township music for the small waiting group. Still, there was never any trouble at that shebeen, so what odds did it make?

8

Summer was over and the last chance of a good rain gone until after the winter. The drought was getting on everyone's nerves. I thought it must even have had an effect on Alan's older brother, Bobby, because he moved out of the Gerbers' house and into lodgings somewhere in Parktown.

"Why does he want to move?" I asked Alan, on the day of Bobby's departure.

"He wants his own independence," Alan said. "He's tired of having my father telling him what to do."

"Really?" I said, astonished at the thought that there was anything less than perfect friendliness between the members of the Gerber household.

"He's been having lots of arguments with my dad."

"Really? He doesn't look the sort to me."

"Who? My dad or Bobby?"

"Both."

"They both enjoy a good scrap, that's for sure. Bobby thinks you have to put your words into action. It's not enough to just talk about the Africans being underprivileged. Everyone should do something about it. My dad says you can't change the world on your own. If you try, it will just lead to trouble."

"You must be sorry he's leaving," I said.

"No," Alan said, breaking into a smile. "I'll move upstairs into his room. It's much bigger than mine and it's got a better view."

"You're heartless," I said. "He's your brother!"

"He's only moving to Parktown, not overseas."

Alan concentrated on his painting for a while. He was doing this portrait of me in his room. He wouldn't let me see it until it was finished, so I didn't know if he was any good as an artist or not.

"You know what we cut up last week?" he asked me.

"No idea," I said.

"A rat!"

"You're kidding me."

"I'm not, man. It was a huge white rat, with this thick pink tail. It was the most revolting thing I ever saw. It was just like that film *What Ever Happened to Baby Jane* with Bette Davis, where she brings in this silver dish on a tray, and when Joan Crawford lifts the lid there's this rat for dinner."

"Sis!" I said.

"I only made one incision into my rat's belly," Alan said.

"And then what?"

"And then I went to town and saw *The Seven Faces of Dr. Lao.*"

"Who's Dr. Lao?" I asked, never having heard of that film.

"He's this Chinese magician who shows every person in this small town the truth about themselves. He shows them all how false their lives are, except for this child who believes in him."

"How are you going to be a doctor if you can't cut up a rat?" I asked.

"That's what I wonder myself," Alan said. "I far prefer to watch a good film."

Bobby came in to say good-bye. He had his guitar hanging over his neck, with a strap decorated with Ndebele beadwork.

"You two must come and visit me, won't you?"

"Sure," Alan said, trying unsuccessfully to hide his painting of me.

Bobby looked over his shoulder and winked at me. "She doesn't look like that. She's much nicer," he teased.

"Why don't you get going?" Alan moaned. "I want to move my things upstairs."

"I don't know what you see in my brother," Bobby said, giving me a hug.

We stood by as Bobby said good-bye to Donnay and to his mother and father.

"Don't worry, I'll keep in touch. And I'll be back every week, Ma, for your food. You know I couldn't survive without that."

"Take care of yourself, Bobby," his father said. "We'll bring over the rest of your things on Tuesday night."

"You take care too, Dad."

Outside, little Sam was hanging upside down from the branch of the mulberry tree.

"Come here, Sammie!" Bobby shouted. "I'm going now. Don't you want to say good-bye?"

"No! You're a pooraboozair!"

"Come here! I've got something for you."

"What's it?"

"I can't say until you come here."

"No, you're only saying that to make me come there."

"Look, Ruth," Bobby said, showing me an imaginary parcel in his hand. "Haven't I got something here for Sammie?"

"Yes!" I said. "He has got something for you here."

"You're a terrible liar!" Bobby whispered to me, as Sam came running across the lawn.

"What is it?" he asked.

"Close your eyes and open your hands!" Bobby said.

Little Sam closed his eyes and opened his dirty hands, palms up. He looked so innocent waiting there for this nonexistent present.

But just when I thought Bobby was taking his joke too far, he put his hand deep in his pocket and pulled out his mouth organ. He laid it in the little chap's hands.

Sam opened his eyes.

"Jeez thanks, Bobby! Don't you want it anymore?"

Sam threw his arms around Bobby and hugged him tightly. Bobby lifted him off the ground and held him there, suspended.

"Yeah, I still want it. But I want you to have it, so that you can play good tunes."

When he was back on terra firma, Sam put the mouth organ in his mouth and sucked in and blew out a few funny sounds.

"You can play this thing, hey?" Bobby said.

"It's puddysticks," Sam said.

"Cherrio, Woodenhead!" Bobby said to the dog, who was leaping up at him. "You look after this family, hey!"

Bobby revved up his old Borgward Isabella with its

bashed front wing where he had once hit a cow on the way to Potchefstroom. He reversed a bit around the pond where Oenk, Poenk, and Stoenk were swimming obliviously, and then he was off down the drive, with us all waving.

Later that morning, I heard Mr. Gerber singing in the lounge. I went to the doorway and looked in.

"Come in, Ruth!" he said. "This song's from *The Man of La Mancha.*"

When he was Bobby's age Mr. Gerber had trained to be an opera singer. He nearly-nearly went to America to further his career as a tenor, but then at the last minute stayed behind to help his father, the general, run a sweet shop for nonwhite people in Port Elizabeth.

His voice was beautiful, if you like Mario Lanza and that kind of singing. I didn't particularly, but I liked Mr. Gerber's singing because I knew him, and he sang with a lot of feeling and used his hands like a proper opera singer.

That morning he sang about dreaming the impossible dream, bearing the unbearable sorrow, righting the unrightable wrong, and going where no one has gone before. It nearly made me cry, because I knew he was singing about Bobby.

9

The van was stacked to the roof with Marienbajam, nature's cure for constipation; Enos, when eating brings discomfort, Enos brings relief; Dr. Williams' Pink Pills, the vitalizing iron tonic; and Sanatogen, which your nerves are hungry for.

Steve was sober for a change. And he was actually talking to his new girlfriend, Rae. From the fascinating bits of conversation I overheard, he was trying to impress her with descriptions of his karate skills.

"So when are you going out again with Cyril?" Alan suddenly whispered to me.

I wondered what made him come up with that question. He must be clairvoyant or something to have known that I was thinking of it. Cyril had been phoning me regularly every week and pleading with me to come out with him. He made out like I was the only girl he really fancied, and I suppose I was flattered. But I did have my doubts: I didn't want to go out with anyone who hung about with black prostitutes in Hillbrow.

"What makes you think I'm going out with him again?"

"Just asking," Alan said, cryptically.

Alan's jealousy was a thing that could easily get on your nerves if you let it. He seemed to worry perpetually about whether I would leave him for someone else. But we weren't going steady; I was under no obligation to him.

"I might go out with him again if he asks me."

"You wouldn't really, would you?"

"Why not? I like him."

Alan's mouth turned down at the edges with disappointment.

"So you'd really go out with him?"

Alan was getting on my nerves all right.

"Yes, of course I would. Why not?"

"Oh, I just wondered if you knew he was homosexual."

I looked straight at Alan.

"What are you talking about, Alan? Why would he go out with me if he's a homosexual? And what about Rhona? I bet Rhona has never been out with a homosexual in her life."

"I'll bet you she has. She went out with Cyril, didn't she?"

"Why does he go out with girls then if he's a homosexual?" I asked. "And what was he doing that night in Hillbrow with the African prostitute?"

"I'm telling you, for sure, he is homosexual."

"How do you know?" I asked, because everything I knew about Cyril made me seriously doubt what Alan was claiming.

"Do you really want to know?" he asked.

I nodded yes.

"You want all the details?"

I nodded again.

"OK then. Last night we worked late at the library, and he brought me home in his old jalopy. And we stopped off at Nitebeat and he asked me if I thought Gary Burne wasn't the handsomest man I'd ever seen."

"So he asked me that, too. But just because a chap likes ballet doesn't make him queer, does it?"

"No, but Cyril actually fancies Gary Burne. Anyway, that's not the whole story. Because then he took me home. But he stopped on the way. Do you know where? Linksfield Ridge. And do you know who was in the car? Just me and him. So why do you think he stopped there?"

"Don't tell me he fancies you as well?" I asked, giggling a bit.

"Well, actually, that's right. He leaned over to me and asked me did I ever have homosexual tendencies. So I told him about things I did when I was younger with other boys. Just ordinary things, not homosexual, but just finding out about how boys worked. Anyway, Cyril obviously got himself worked up, because he said he was sure I must be homosexual too, and would I like to try out kissing with him."

"Are you serious, Alan? I know I'm very gullible, and I'll believe all this if you tell me it's true."

"On my mother's life," he said.

"You shouldn't swear on your mother's life, or on anyone's," I said, but I knew from his oath that he wasn't spinning me a line.

"It's true. He wanted to kiss me. But first of all, I'm not homosexual. And secondly, even if I was, I wouldn't fancy Cyril. He's not my sort of person at all."

"God, Alan," I said. "Why did he go out with me? Why didn't he tell me? Now it means that I've kissed a homosexual. That's disgusting."

"Ruth! Don't be so prejudiced," Alan said. "There's nothing wrong with him, you know."

"Well, if he only likes blokes, why does he go with black prostitutes then?"

"I didn't ask him. Maybe he's trying to make up his mind."

10

Every year Mannie used to go to the Durban July. Of course, it wasn't to watch his horse Kubla Khan race; there was no connection whatsoever between Kubla Khan and the Durban July. The only way that poor specimen of a horse would ever have finished the Durban July would have been if it started the race in January.

But Mannie enjoyed the occasion of the Durban July and used it as an excuse for one of his two annual holidays. The way he liked it was to go down by train a week in advance and stay at the King Edward Hotel. Then Ullman would fly down the day before the race and spend a long weekend in Durban.

That was always the best couple of weeks in the year for Mom and me. We got on fabulously when he was away. Mom relaxed out, and her nerves restored themselves to some kind of balance just in time for his return. Then, within twenty-four hours, for sure, she would be back to her jittery self again. It was tragic to watch the whole transformation.

As the Durban July approached, a plan was formulating in my head to have a party at my house. My birthday's only in August, but I was prepared to have an early party, because in August Mannie would be back and I'd have no chance. I had never had one before because of Mannie's habits and need for deadly silence. But while he was away there would be no sock hung out on the bedroom handle, and he need never even know about the party.

I asked Lenore what she thought the chances were.

"You know Mom doesn't like music," she said. "She's never let me have a party when I've asked for one."

But I had a feeling that the time was right to approach her on this issue.

"Mom, did I tell you that Mr. Gerber nearly was an opera singer?" I said to her one night in the breakfast room.

I thought subtlety was my best chance of introducing the subject.

"Really?" Mom said, without looking up from the paperwork she was doing. "Has he got a good voice?"

"Excellent. I've heard him sing 'Ol' Man River' and 'To Dream the Impossible Dream.' He really sings well."

I still hadn't managed to catch Mom's attention.

"Their whole family is quite musical. Bobby plays the guitar, and even their old granny sings songs from her childhood."

Mom stopped writing. At last, I thought she was going to give me my opportunity. But she just screwed up her face.

"What's wrong?" I asked her.

"I just remembered this case that Percy Zlotkin is working on. Apparently this farmer put an African's hands in a vise and then beat him to death with a sjambok."

"Sis, Mom. Why do you tell me these things?"

"Because they're true and they happened and I can't forget them."

Mom got back to her work. I decided to abandon subtlety—it could take all night.

"Listen, Mom, please. I'd like to have a party here."

That got Mom looking up at me all right.

"How can you? Mannie would hate it. Please don't start any more trouble."

"I've thought it all out," I told her. "We have the party when he's away for the Durban July."

I could see Mom thumbing through all the excuses in her head.

"But what about the carpets in the lounge? It will make such a mess."

"John can move them out before the party. And there won't be such a mess. We don't have to have much food."

"But what about the neighbors? Mrs. Levine hardly gets a night's rest as it is."

"It's only one night in the year. All my friends have parties."

Mom was suffering; I could see it. But she wouldn't come right out and say it, so I said it for her.

"It's the music, isn't it? Why don't you say so?"

"OK, Ruthie. It is the music."

"Mom, you can't go on avoiding music all your life. The Jewish custom is no music for one year, not twelve! You can't mourn forever."

Mom was on the point of sobbing. It was pitiful, and I wanted to comfort her.

"Come on, Mom! What is so wrong about music? It's not a crime."

"You don't understand, Ruthie. You don't understand."

11

The house Bobby lived in was an old farmhouse. It had flaking whitewashed walls, and the garden had gone to seed—literally. It was a jungle of weeds. He shared the house with several other people, male and female, some of whom were students, but others looked to me like Bohemians or beatniks or something like that.

"Nobody bothers what we get up to here," Bobby told us. "It suits me just fine."

His bedroom didn't look all that different from his previous one. There were books everywhere, on shelves and in piles on the floor. But it wasn't untidy. Bobby knew where every book was in that room. He had been settled in for about three weeks before Alan and I went to visit him. Mr. Gerber dropped us there but didn't stay long himself. Bobby told his father that he would bring us home in the Isabella.

Bobby made us dinner in the communal kitchen. It was a simple meal: fried chops, eggs, and salad, which we ate off this old wooden table. A bloke called Greg with a huge black beard joined us halfway through, had a coffee, asked us if we heard that the Beatles had been awarded an MBE, and then left as suddenly as he had come.

"And for afters," Bobby joked, "melon and homemade ice cream."

We tucked into the sweet orange flesh of the fruit smothered with chocolate ice cream.

Bobby was really interested to know how his family was getting on since he'd left home. Alan told him all the latest about their parents and about Donnay and little Sam.

"So, Ruth, I hear you also left home," Bobby said, when we'd returned to his bedroom.

"Yes, but I only went to my relations."

"Of course, yes," Bobby said. "Where else could you go? But next time you could come here if you want. The rent is very cheap."

"Who'll pay her rent?" Alan said. He didn't sound very keen on the idea.

"No, seriously," Bobby said. "Think about it. Everybody needs their own headspace."

"Thanks," I said. "But my mom couldn't handle it. She's very nervous."

Later in the evening we heard a double knock on Bobby's door at the same time as it opened.

When I saw the head pop round the door I thought it must be a houseboy or someone looking for work.

"Howzit, Ben!" Bobby said, jumping up and clapping his own hand against the African's hand. "Come in, man. This is my brother, Alan, and this is his girlfriend, Ruth, and this is Ben, a good pal of mine."

I was flabbergasted! Ben was a black bloke about Bobby's age, or maybe a year or two older.

I felt so awkward, never having been in such a situation before. I didn't know whether to put out a hand or not. It was the first time a black person ever offered to shake my hand on equal terms.

"Howzit, Alan . . . Ruth," he said, shaking each of our hands in turn.

"You're the one studying medicine, aren't you?" Ben said to Alan, who nodded.

"Yes, but I hate it," Alan said. "I'm not cut out for that sort of thing."

"So why did you do it?"

"Because it's expected of a nice Jewish boy. I had to do law or medicine or accountancy. What else? But I'm no good at cutting up bits of body."

"Bobby did politics. Why didn't you choose something you wanted to do?"

It was a good question that Ben asked. I had never thought to ask Alan why he chose medicine.

"Because my folks weren't at all pleased with Bobby's choice, and for years they gave me all this propaganda about not following in his footsteps."

"Well, parents get stuck in their old ways," he said.

"Mine believe that the white people will govern this country forever."

Alan looked thoughtful.

"I was never as strong-willed as Bobby," he said. "I compromise much more than he does; he sticks to his principles."

"Well, you're much younger," Bobby said, opening a couple of cans of Castle lager and a Coke for me. "You don't have to think about principles till you're older. Then you'll make up your own mind. And you can always learn from mistakes. If medicine isn't right for you, you can always change."

"Ja, everyone must do what they can," Ben said.

He asked me if I was still at school, and I told him I was in my final year.

"And what will you do when you matriculate?" he asked me.

"Go to Wits, I suppose," I said.

"To study what?"

"I don't know. B.A. maybe."

He looked at me in a funny sort of way.

"You're not speaking too much. Are you frightened of me being here? Don't worry! It's OK, as long as nobody does anything illegal."

"Why should I be frightened?" I asked.

"Some white girls are frightened. They grow up paranoid of us guys."

I must have looked troubled because he suddenly broke out into a smile.

"Hey, it's OK. Bobby, tell her that I haven't been living with baboons all my life."

Bobby smiled.

"I don't tell lies!" he said.

Ben burst into a laugh, and I could see that the two of them must have understood each other pretty well, because white people and Africans didn't usually go in for that sort of humoring.

Later they started talking politics. Alan joined in, but mostly I just listened.

"First it was fourteen days' detention without trial," Bobby said. "Then ninety. Then a hundred and eighty. Now it's unlimited so long as they get authorization from a judge."

"What's next?" Ben said. "No authorization, I suppose."

"How can judges agree to a thing that goes against the principles of justice?" Alan asked.

"Judges aren't there for justice," Ben answered. "They just make the system workable."

"Even the minister of justice is not interested in justice," Bobby said. "That Vorster has got a big chip on his shoulder because he was detained for twenty months during the Second World War."

"What for?" I asked.

"For supporting the Nazis," Bobby explained. "Now he wants to get his revenge by putting as many people as he can into detention."

"Ja, the two big Vs," Ben said. "Verwoerd and Vorster. They think they can hold back our people for ever. Aikona!"

"And what about Feinberg?" Bobby asked.

I discovered that Feinberg was apparently found dead in his bathroom the day before.

"Who was he?" I asked.

"He was doing a five-year sentence under the Suppression of Communism Act," Ben explained.

"The police said he committed suicide in his own bathroom," Bobby said.

"No way!" Ben said. "They killed him for sure."

At about eleven o'clock, Bobby drove us home in the Isabella.

As Ben climbed into the backseat with Alan, he winked at me and said, "If the police stop us, you can say I'm your new garden boy."

12

A month before the Durban July, Sea Cottage, the most valuable horse in the country, was shot while he was training on the beach at Blue Lagoon.

Mannie was among those who would have backed Sea Cottage, and he was upset by the news.

"What maniac would go and shoot a horse?" he said. "Who am I going to back now?"

Then he read in a newspaper that an African diviner in Pietersburg had tickled the throat of a chicken in order to look into the future, and guess what? The man saw Sea Cottage running the race and doing well!

Mannie was overjoyed when he heard Sea Cottage was going to run in the race after all, even though it still had the sniper's bullet lodged in its hindquarters. He was convinced that it would win, and he put a lot of money on it.

Of course, it lost out to Java Head, which won the race

in record time. Poor old Sea Cottage was doing well, just like the tickled chicken said, but then it was accidentally bumped by another horse.

13

My party was a great success from most points of view. I think the only one who didn't enjoy it was Alan. But then I had always told Alan that he took our relationship too seriously.

Mom kept a low profile at the party. She had refused to go out for the evening as I suggested. Instead she did her work in the breakfast room with the door closed. But she kept on making surprise appearances throughout the evening.

By nine o'clock everything was in full swing. There were couples dancing and most of the food was already eaten, and most of what remained was on the floor. But at least John had rolled up the carpets in the afternoon and moved them into another room.

Alan came with Merv in the van. Adele looked gorgeous, I must admit, in this new frock she had on.

The whole evening she held on to Merv's hand until I began to worry that she had sewn herself to him.

Steve was there with a new girlfriend who looked much older than us lot. It turned out she was a pharmacy student Steve had met on the Wits campus. Her name was Tamara, and she wouldn't let anyone call her Tammy. Steve had made headway into the bottle of Gordon's Dry, and I just hoped Mom wouldn't notice it on one of her snoop missions. When I was introduced to Tamara, I noticed that she also reeked of Gordon's Dry. Perhaps the smell was contagious.

Cyril came as well, and with a girl I knew. I made pleasant conversation with him and didn't mention the words "homo" or "prostitute" once. He looked so comfortable in the company of girls, I couldn't bring myself to believe what Alan had told me about him. What on earth his bigshot father must have thought of him, I couldn't imagine.

Alan was annoyed with me for talking so much to Cyril, so I deliberately spoke more to him. Alan got niggly about it, then pretended he didn't care much what I did. He went over to Steve and Tamara and joined in the boozing.

My friend Merle supplied most of the records. She had lots of hit songs by Elvis and the Beatles and the Rolling Stones and the Dave Clark Five, but she also had good dance music like Dan Hill, Ray Conniff, Perry Como, and Frank Sinatra. She was going steady with this boy Michael Dreyer who used to live on the next street. I knew Michael well in those days because he was the first boy who ever asked me to go steady. I was seven at the time. He had grown up a lot since those days, and I suppose so had I, except in a certain two unmentionable places.

Later, I saw Alan go up to Lenore while her boyfriend, Hilton, was in the kitchen. He was chatting and laughing with her. The cheek of it! She was my younger sister, and I only let her come to the party out of sisterly feeling—and some persuasion from Mom. Mind you, she looked as old as I did, and probably she was prettier than all the rest of us put together, except maybe Adele.

I went over and grabbed Alan and started dancing with him. It was "Yesterday" by the Beatles, and it was Alan's favorite song. But it was like dancing with the Leaning Tower of Pisa: he was very drunk and had to use me as a support. It became very tiring, and I was just about to say something nasty about it during one slow dance, when he pulled out this box from his pocket and gave it to me with a Happy Birthday sloppy kiss. It was a silver ring with a semiprecious stone set in the middle.

"It's an iger's tie," he said, clumsily sliding it on my finger. Of course, I understood his drunk tongue was trying to say "tiger's eye."

For the rest of the dance I let him put his cheek against mine which caused Merv to whistle at us as he and Adele drifted past. While Alan's cheek was there, he suggested for the five hundred thousandth time that we go steady.

"We've been going out since New Year's Day, haven't we?" he said. "That's how many months?"

He tried to count the months but got stuck at March.

"You're drunk, Alan," I said.

"I'm not," he said. "April, March, May . . . How many's that?"

"It's about six months," I said.

"So why won't you go steady with me?" he pleaded.

"Because," I said, pulling away my cheek from his.

I hated anyone who ever said "because" to me, so that's probably why I said it to Alan—I knew it would annoy him.

"Don't just say 'because,' " he said. "Surely you've got a reason."

"I have," I said. "Because this is my party, and I can dance with other boys if I want to."

"They've all got someone to dance with. They don't want you."

"Oh, don't they?" I said.

To prove the point I asked Cyril to dance, even though his partner looked daggers at me, and after Cyril I asked Michael Dreyer, and my best friend Merle wasn't too pleased with me either, and after Michael Dreyer I saw Alan leave the room holding his head. I followed him out and suggested he lie down for a while.

I hesitated about letting him into my room because, as my Mom said, I didn't take pride in it. I could have let him into Lenore's room, which was a model of prettiness with its white furniture and the tapestries she had made herself, but I settled for my room and lay him down on my bed.

"You have a rest," I said, fingering the ring he had given me and feeling sorry that I'd been off-putting to him.

"Is that wallpaper crooked," he asked, "or are my eyes crooked?"

I closed the door and went back to the party.

Merv and Adele were still dancing together, if you could call it dancing. It was more like an octopus imitation with tentacles interlocked.

Steve and Tamara were sitting on our couch with Merle and Michael. I could hear Steve going on about something. I guessed it was sport.

"I was forty-six not out and going well. I had got the hang of their best bowler and decided a four would be the best way to bring up my fifty."

His hands were gesturing every stroke he was talking about.

"Then this bowler let fly. It was perfect for a square drive. I positioned my feet, then swung the bat round. . . ."

He demonstrated the whole movement vividly, tipping what was left of the Gordon's Dry over Tamara's dress.

"God, Steve! Look what you've done! Who cares about your batting?" Tamara wasn't pleased. She tried to dry the mess with a paper serviette and went off in a huff.

"Did you get the boundary?" Michael asked.

"No, the ball must have hit a stone or something. It couldn't have spun that much."

"You mean you were out?"

"Yes, for forty-six. Still, it was the highest score on our side."

Steve stood up and caught sight of his reflection in the wall mirror. He brushed his hair back and pouted his lips the way he always did to check that he was still good-looking.

"I better go find Tamara or she'll stick pins in my effigy."

He could hardly stand up on his own and staggered out of the room in the direction of the bathroom.

Soon after that, I heard this bit of a rumpus on the veranda.

"What's going on out there?" I asked Merle.

"Gate-crashers," she said.

"How many?"

"Three couples."

"Oh God," I said. "There's already too many people in here."

"Merv is talking to them," Merle said.

I looked out of the lounge window.

"Come on, man, be a sport," one gate-crasher was saying.

"If we let you in," Merv said, "then we'd have to let in every gate-crasher."

"I don't see any others. There's just us. Come on, man, be a sport. It's cold out here."

"No. It's very full inside."

Through the window I had a good view of them. They were very smartly dressed and didn't look like trouble. So I shouted through the window to Merv that they could come in.

The one with the white sports jacket caught my eye immediately.

"Thanks for letting us in," he said. "I'm Larry." And he introduced me to his girlfriend, and to his two buddies, Phil and Alwyn.

Larry had these light-green eyes, so light that even in the semidarkness they looked transparent. I had never seen such eyes ever on a bloke.

He and his crew joined in the party, and they mingled well with our lot. But after a while Larry came over to me alone, leaving his girlfriend talking to the others.

"Why aren't you dancing with anyone?" he asked me. His light-green eyes melted me.

"My partner's not feeling well," I explained. "He's lying down."

"Do you think he'd mind if I danced with you?"

"Probably he would," I said.

"But it's a shame not to dance at your own party," he said. His eyes were very persuasive.

"OK," I said.

He began to dance with me immediately and explained that it wasn't a proper gate-crash, because one of his friends was a friend of Michael Dreyer.

"What did you get in matric?" I asked him.

"A first."

Very good, I thought.

"Distinctions in any subject?" I asked.

"No. I got a B, though, in history."

Not so good, I thought.

"What do you do now?" I asked.

"First-year law."

I suppose that will do, I thought. I was satisfied.

"What's your surname?"

"Malamud."

Now Mom would be satisfied too.

"Run out of questions?" he said, smiling.

When the dance ended, he didn't release me. So I said, "Shouldn't you get back to your girlfriend?" and he said, "Just another dance."

We danced together for what seemed like hours, and during that time he did most of the talking. He was a good talker, and I liked the sound of his voice and the things he was telling me. I learned that he had just turned eighteen and been given an Austin Healey for his birthday, that his family was exceedingly wealthy, with a mansion of some sort in Mountainview; and that his father owned Phoenix Electroplating.

After a number of slow dances I began to feel sorry for his girlfriend, although she seemed happy enough making new acquaintances. As far as I was concerned, though, there was definitely something electric happening between me and Larry. I could especially feel it when he steered me toward the back wall behind the partition and began to press against me.

That first kiss made me realize why I had never wanted to go steady with Alan.

Larry's light-green eyes were very fascinating. His hair was straw colored: not quite blond, not quite brown either. He was very well-built. He told me that he liked to keep in good shape because he was a competitive swimmer and was also keen on mountaineering. It was easy to tell that he was a good athlete, and I must admit, I could feel my heart pounding a bit with his body so close.

But unfortunately Alan chose just this moment to come charging through the smooching couples in our direction. I don't know if someone tipped him off or if he just woke up from his drunken stupor.

I felt sorry for Alan; he looked so miserable. I thought now at least he'll know what it was like for Erroll Pinkus on New Year's Eve when Erroll found Alan and me kissing under the grapevine.

But I didn't think it was a good time to remind Alan of the similarity—he wasn't in the mood for comparisons.

"What's going on, Ruth?" he said. "I was only taking a rest."

"Sorry, Alan. This is Larry."

"I don't care who he is. Leave him alone!"

"You can't tell me what to do."

"Can't I?" Alan screamed.

"Don't yell at her!" Larry said, which made Alan wilder than ever.

"If you don't leave go of him, it's over between us."

"OK then," I said. "If that's the way you want it."

"I don't want it that way," he shouted, "but you obviously do."

Mom's head poked round the door.

"This is Larry Malamud," I said to her, making sure she heard the good Jewish surname before she saw how close our good Jewish bodies were to each other.

"Is everything all right, Ruthie?"

"Sure, Mom."

Mom's puzzled head disappeared.

"Give me back my ring!" Alan said.

I handed over the ring with the tiger's eye in it, and Alan stormed out of the house.

"That was my boyfriend," I said to Larry.

"I would never have guessed," he said.

PART FIVE

1

THE MALAMUDS' HOUSE HAD TWO OF EV-erything, and where it didn't have two of everything it had three of everything, except for servants, of which there were four. The house had two stories, two stairways, two lounges overlooking the gardens, two swimming pools, two sprinklers, three Doberman pinschers, three bathrooms, three toilets, and three garages, each occupied by a smart car.

You could tell Mr. Malamud was into silver-plating in a big way. The taps were silver-plated, the chandeliers were silver-plated, the ornaments poking out from every display cabinet were silver-plated, the cutlery was silver-plated of course, and I was only surprised that the palm trees in the garden weren't silver-plated.

I thought Uncle Harry P-chinsky was well off until I met the Malamuds—they were simply in a different league. But these people weren't deliberately ostentatious. They wore their wealth quite naturally, the way a peacock wears its tail.

But they were nice enough. Take Mrs. Malamud, for instance. She had no need to work, of course not, but worked hard entertaining women from this organization and that organization. And Larry's sister, Raselle, had no need to work, because she could have found someone to marry her even if she had the brains of a zongalulu and looked like the back of a lorry. But she worked part-time at Phoenix Electroplating in the reception area, which a zongalulu couldn't have done, could it? And what's more she didn't look like the back of a lorry either. Though from the way Larry spoke, you'd think she'd had a nose like an eagle's beak before her operation.

"Are you related to the Hirsches in the Jaguar business?" Mr. Malamud said when I was introduced to him.

I didn't know if he meant cars or jungle animals, but as our family were in neither business, I said no.

"A pity," he said, walking off, probably to go and silver-plate the front door.

Actually the front door was a sight to behold. It had these two white pillars on either side of it like a Greek temple or something. And these two pillars supported what looked like an upstairs veranda. I bet from there you would have had a good view of the front garden. Well, it wasn't a garden—it was more like a province. It stretched in all directions, and the main swimming pool and the baby pool were hardly noticeable among the trees and rockeries and fountains and summerhouses.

I felt sorry for Larry's Austin Healey though. There wasn't any garage space for it, and he had to park it outside where the rain would have got at it if it wasn't the middle of the biggest drought in fifty years.

Mind you, it didn't look like the Malamuds had heard of the drought. Their shrubberies were luxuriant even in the middle of winter.

As for the two lounges, they each had a glass wall on one side so that you could get a panoramic view of the garden no matter which lounge you were in. Of course, it crossed my mind that no person could sit in two lounges at any one time, but obviously it was necessary in that family to have a good choice of atmosphere. One lounge consisted entirely of antiques, including the Persian carpet on the floor. The other lounge was totally different with bulky African modern-art sculptures standing around like they were guests at a buffet party. These were real art sculptures, not like the tourist trash Mannie went in for. This room had an African-design carpet on the highly polished parquet floor.

I never had the choice to go in either room, so I couldn't tell you about their atmosphere. I just peeked in once or twice. I got the impression only special guests were allowed in those rooms, because of the priceless carpets, and anyhow the furniture was covered with white sheets most of the time, so where would anyone have sat?

The family preferred the sunroom for everyday use, and I was allowed in there to help myself from the most fantastic display of crystalized fruit I ever saw in my life. It was arranged according to the colors of the fruit, on a huge circular tray on a glass table.

"Take a few, Ruth," Mrs. Malamud said. She was dressed in a black-and-white op-art dress that shimmered with visual illusions. Lines that seemed curved were in fact straight, and when you looked closely, the circular designs were in fact as square as chessboards. A dress like that must have cost a fortune!

The mound of fruit was immaculate, with spirals of pineapple, watermelon, mango, lemon, peach, and so on. It was at least two feet in diameter and nearly as tall. I think they were expecting guests there that night, judging from Mrs. Malamud's dress—I hope so, because otherwise someone had gone to a lot of trouble for nothing. I chose a piece of orange because it was at the summit, and I was scared to take anything from a lower level in case the whole mountain collapsed.

Larry's friends were also well-off. Alwyn's father had something to do with gold mining. By the way Alwyn splashed his money around, I wouldn't have been at all surprised if he owned City Deep or something.

Take the night we all went gambling. First Alwyn and Larry had this argument about whose car to go in, and in the end Alwyn persuaded us to go in his Alfa Romeo Giulietta Sprint.

He drove us at high speed to Kotze Street in Hillbrow, flashing his lights at any girls he laid eyes on. His girlfriend Arlene must have been used to it, because she didn't punch him in the jaw or anything.

He took us to this neon-lit building and led us through the L-shaped foyer and down a set of steps to this door that had a slit of glass at eye level, though covered from the inside with a piece of cardboard.

Alwyn knocked on the door. The cardboard was slid across, and this black man's eyes looked out at us. The door opened an inch. Alwyn mentioned the name of a certain Mr. Toffee Sharp, and we were let in. Alwyn was like that; he had lots of connections in Joburg.

I had never been in a gambling den before. It was so smoky you could hardly see the beans that the Chinaman was counting into piles of four. Anyhow, he did it so fast that you got the feeling that his blurred fingers were persuading those beans into piles of four without even touching them.

Alwyn lost 127 rand at his first attempt. This is how he did it. He started off with a pencil and paper because he had been shown this foolproof method of winning money. He ticked off all the numbers that came up, and watched out for a number that hadn't come up for a long time. The numbers were pretty even for a while, but then the number three started lagging behind.

Alwyn started getting excited when three hadn't come up six times in a row. By the time it reached eight times in a row he couldn't sit still and his hand went for his pocket.

"One rand on number three!"

Of course by then, three had got into the habit of not coming up so Alwyn won nothing. But now he put into action phase two of his plan.

"Two rand on number three!"

Three was still reluctant to get itself chosen, so Alwyn doubled again. The idea was that as long as you doubled, the number had to come up in the end and then you'd win back everything you'd staked before.

"Four rand!"

"Eight rand!"

"Sixteen rand!"

"Thirty-two rand!"

"Sixty-four rand!"

At this point Alwyn began to suspect that the China-man's fingers were doing more than just persuading those beans. Although he handled them so nonchalantly, that Chinaman looked like he could easily turn a group of three beans into a group of four without so much as a blink.

Alwyn chickened out and stopped betting.

The number three didn't come up next time, but it did the time after. So if he'd put on another 384 rand, he would have cleaned up. But who knows? That number might have been even more reluctant to show itself if Alwyn had betted extra money.

I'm not saying nobody won in that place. A lot of the small-time gamblers won five rand here or ten rand there. And I saw with my own eyes a bloke haul in 300 rand in one go. But I also saw this woman in furs who arrived with two men, one of whom looked like he'd got out of *The Dirty Dozen* and was bald as an egg. When the baldy helped the lady take off her furs, she had on this lemony dress with satin embroidery which showed up her tan fabulously.

She didn't use Alwyn's foolproof method. Hers was more intuitive. She just thought of a number and then put a hundred rand on it. She did this ten times, lost ten times, then asked the baldy to help her on with her furs, and then she left. One thousand rand gone in half an hour. Not bad! It made Alwyn feel a stack better.

We didn't leave after Alwyn's first loss. Both Larry and Phil continued with small bets here and there, neither of them gaining or losing much. Alwyn tried again later, but I didn't see how much he lost because by then I was absorbed in watching the two policemen who were visiting.

Their visit was so important that a bow-tied Chinaman emerged from somewhere and showed them round. One of the things he showed them was a bottle of whisky and the other thing was a roll of rand notes bound together by a piece of string. The policemen couldn't be tempted to stay longer—obviously they had seen enough for one night.

It struck me that those policemen couldn't have shared the government's scorn for Chinese people. That night they treated them exactly as they would have treated Japanese business partners.

Afterward I wondered if that Chinaman was the famous Chong who ran the fah-fee in our neighborhood. It could have been, but then again, there must be a lot of China-men in Joburg.

2

Whenever I went to the Malamuds, which was quite often in the first month of our relationship, Larry entertained me in the leisure room which came off the snooker room via glass double doors.

It was there that I learned to chalk the cue and cue the ball. It was there that I learned that the silver-plated trophies on the mantelpiece hadn't been won by anybody—they were just more ornaments to make the room look good. And it was there that I could have learned the facts of life because Larry was sexually very experienced.

He told me all about this group of nurses he knew. In fact, he seemed to know a lot more about nurses than

Alan's crew of medical students. I think he liked their uniforms, because he seemed to have spent more of his life with those nurses than in the law library. From what I could make out, he liked those nurses' uniforms even more when the nurses were undressed out of them.

But Larry didn't try to take advantage of me all at once; he played his cards quite slowly. But I knew I was up against the real thing, especially when he continued his habit of pressing me up against a wall in a romantic corner of a dark room. I didn't mind that so much, as long as there were lots of other people around. But that leisure room was dangerous. I had a strong conviction that Larry wasn't the sort of person who would like to find out that his girl was more padding than flesh. So I avoided that room like it was a torture chamber.

In fact, I soon started to avoid Larry's house altogether. Especially when he got to know me well enough to divulge that his mother had also had a nose job done on her some years ago. It struck me that the male Malamuds were very into appearances, and anything they didn't like, they changed to suit their own tastes. And probably the same applied to breasts. In fact, I had wondered if Mrs. Malamud and daughter had also had silicone jobs done, but of course I couldn't ever broach that subject with Larry; it was an untouchable as far as I was concerned, and that's the way I wanted my breasts to remain too. As long as Larry thought I looked good, that was enough for me. I wanted to be his girl, maybe even go steady with him, so long as we avoided the leisure activities.

However, it was inevitable, I suppose, with a dishy bloke like Larry that my luck would run out.

It happened on the night of my real birthday when he

took me dancing at the Stables. We went there with two of his friends and their dates, and Larry and I sat out one dance. It must have been the way the candlelight flickered over our faces, that he got this urgent look on his face.

"Ruth," he said.

"Larry," I said.

"Seriously," he said. "I've got you a birthday present."

He produced this pearl necklace, which proved to me that my luck was beginning to run out because I don't like necklaces. But one thing, it must have cost a bomb. These pearls were the real dinkum McCoy. In the candlelight they had that real-pearl quality that makes a girl obliged to any bloke who gives her such a thing. If money could talk, then those pearls were giving a lecture.

Of course I had to wear those pearls for the rest of the night, which gave him the opportunity to start fingering my neck. Between the glow of those pearls and the glow of his transparent green eyes, I was finding myself in a real predicament.

In the end, Larry was the first to speak about it.

"You're holding out on me," he said, as he danced with me. "Aren't you?"

"What do you mean?" I said, all innocence.

"You know. You always avoid me touching you."

"No, I don't. We're dancing close together now, aren't we?"

"Yes, but let's go to my car and get a bit closer."

That was it, I thought. It's probably all over between us now, and it's a shame because I really liked him in a way that I've never liked anybody before. We could have made a great couple.

"I don't want to go to the car," I said. "Can't we just enjoy dancing?"

"What's wrong with you, Ruth? I like you a lot, and we've been going out over a month, but I'm a normal bloke, you know. You can't be so uptight with me all the time. Sometimes you're as cold as ice to me."

As he said that, I got this vivid picture of a young ballerina doing her demicharacter called the "Ice Maiden."

"You must give me time," I said.

"But how much time do you need? I might be qualified by the time you're ready. I can't wait that long."

"If you can't wait a bit more, that's too bad," I said. "I like getting to know someone very well before . . ."

"Come on, Ruth! Don't pretend so much. I know perfectly well that you haven't gone very far with anyone. I don't mind that, honestly. I'm only too happy to be the one who will make you into a real woman."

He shouldn't have said that about a real woman, because I nearly told him there and then to push off out of my life.

"I'm real enough, thank you very much, just as I am. I don't need you or any big shot to make me more real."

"I'm sorry, Ruth. I didn't mean it that way. But you must understand."

"So must you," I said. "Give me time to get to know you better and then we'll see."

"OK," he said, pulling me affectionately toward him like he was fitting a key into a lock, "I'll give you another month, how's that?"

"God, man!" I said, pulling away from his embrace. "Are you going to tick off the days on a calendar? Who do you think you are? One of my teachers?"

"Sorry, Ruth. You always take things the wrong way. I don't mean a month, strictly speaking. I just mean I can't go on like this year after year, or anything."

"So who said anything about years?" I asked.

3

That night I dreamt I was walking down Eloff Street with Mom. We were just passing these pathetic African cripples who sit there on the floor with their deformed legs folded up somewhere near their chests, or with no legs at all sitting on these little box-carts with small wheels so that they can get about, or with stumps of arms and legs wrapped in dirty cloths, or those blind beggars with those signs hanging around their necks saying that they're blind. They're always there on the pavement on Eloff Street begging. Anyhow, Mom gave them each five cents, but then she turned into the OK Bazaar and I didn't see her go in. I called out for her, but she didn't hear. Next thing, this European man came up to me and he said, "You're not wearing Playtex, are you? I can tell a mile off!" and he called a couple of his pals over, and they started laughing. "That's not Maidenform either," one of them said. "It's not a bra! It's falsies!" I tried to cover myself up by crossing my arms, but one of them said, "Shame! She's deformed. She's got no tits at all!" The others all said, "Really? Let's have a squizz!" And they started peeling off my clothes. I ran away from them, but by that time I'm stark naked. "Her titties are so tiny!" one of them shouted after me, "She's not even a real woman!"

My God, I woke up in a state. I felt my body in the dark, and it was just about true what they were saying.

I realized my time was running out with Larry unless my breasts got the message and began to do something within the next month or two. But it was becoming a huge bore having this problem for the rest of my life. I'd have to go through this with every bloke I ever met. I couldn't stand it anymore. I sobbed that night just like Mom.

4

I had been going out with Larry for about seven weeks and had not seen or heard of Alan Gerber. Actually, I hadn't even thought about him. Well, I thought about his family sometimes; I missed going round there. And I missed talking to Bobby because he was the most decent person I had ever known.

But one afternoon I was up at the shops, and who should I see but little Sam on his tricycle. Mrs. Gerber was with him.

"Hello, Ruth," she said. "How are you these days?"

"I'm fine, Mrs. Gerber. And you?"

"We're all well, thank God."

Little Sam got off his tricycle and stood in front of me wobbling his right foot on the side of his heel.

"It's gone all zonky," he said to me.

"He means his bicycle wheel," Mrs. Gerber explained.

"Look at it!" little Sam said, getting on and pedaling down the pavement.

The wheel was very zonky, I had to admit.

"You must tell Alan to fix it," I said to him. Then I said to his mother, "How is Alan?"

"Actually, he's moping around a lot. I don't think he's very happy with what he's doing."

"Well, say hello to him for me," I said, walking on into the shopping center, because the last thing I wanted was to hear a sob story about Alan missing me or something.

5

At long last, the note I was waiting for arrived in the post. It said there was a parcel for me to collect at the post office.

I didn't waste a second getting up there. The section next door for nonwhites was quite full, but there was no one waiting in the main post office for whites, so I was served immediately.

"Ruth Hirsch, that's the one," the man said. "Here's your parcel, lady."

It was wrapped in brown paper and tied with coarse string, but I didn't open it till I got back home.

I locked my bedroom door, closed my venetian blinds, and opened the packaging. There it was at last, exactly as it looked in the Femina advertisement. The Vibr-o-sonic Breast Massager, guaranteed to add inches to your bustline. I read through the instructions very quickly because I couldn't wait to get started adding those inches.

I took off my cardigan, blouse, and padded bra. I thought of kissing the padded bra good-bye and throwing it in the dustbin there and then, but I thought, wait a minute, my bust might not grow enough from just one session.

Anyhow, I lay down on my bed and put these two cups that looked like mattress springs over my breasts and then switched on the machine. It made a constant buzzing noise, and it felt pretty weird, I must admit, like two great bumblebees doing this dance on my body. The instruction leaflet said to start with ten- to twenty-minute sessions, so I thought I'd keep it on for twenty minutes to get maximum effect.

I closed my eyes and relaxed and had these images of my breasts growing until they looked if not like Marilyn Monroe's, then at least like Sandra Dee's. That sort of girl had nothing to worry about. Take Rhona Tabatznik, for example—and many boys had!—she had nothing to worry about, except where she was going to get an education now that she had been expelled. But as far as boys go—and with her, boys went as far as was humanly possible—she had no fears. And even my best friend Merle, though she had nothing like Rhona's gifts, had nothing to be ashamed of.

As I was thinking these thoughts, I could almost feel my breasts growing.

Vibr-o-sonic will do what no cream will ever do! Vibr-o-sonic, the latest in bust development from America! Vibr-o-sonic, as used by Hollywood stars, to bring out the best in you!

I thought my twenty minutes must be nearly up, so I opened my eyes to check my watch. And then I got the fright of my life!

I nearly died of shock! I got goose bumps of fear all over my body!

There were these eyes looking in at me through the

damaged place in my venetian blinds! Eyes, I'm telling you, spying on me!

I nearly died from embarrassment and fear!

As I saw those Peeping-Tom eyes, they quickly turned away.

Oh my God, it was terrible!

It was a man's eyes! And what's more, an African man's eyes! In fact, I could have sworn those eyes belonged to John, our garden boy!

I was hysterical with fear. I wanted to scream, but I was too scared.

I turned away from the window and covered myself. Then I slipped on my blouse, crept to the venetian blinds, and peeped out through the gap.

John was there all right, standing next to the car in the drive as if he were washing it. He was talking to Betty from next door as though he'd been standing there all afternoon. Little Hymie stood next to Betty, beating his crash-helmeted head against the iron fence pole.

My body was shaking like it had caught a chill, and my mind was doing a number on me. I couldn't think straight. It was like one of my nightmares, but I just couldn't wake up from it.

My first thought was to phone the police. They'd teach him a lesson for spying on the young white madam. But then I thought I better let Mom handle it. She was right about him after all—he was nothing better than an animal, I thought. And Betty next door, standing there like an innocent angel protecting her pathetic little white boy, was no better, with her shebeen to encourage immoral behavior. I bet the police would sort it all out.

It was ironic, I thought, that the only white person who

was witness to what had happened to me was little Hymie, locked in his dumb, private world. He would never be able to back me up.

The shame of being spied on was the worst part. Especially because I was so flat-chested. It wouldn't have been half so bad if I had at least something to be proud of. But flat-chested! And having on those ridiculous mattress springs!

And then it dawned on me—how long had he been spying on me? Probably the whole twenty minutes! I couldn't bear the humiliation of it. Sis! It made me want to vomit. Twenty minutes he had probably watched me, with that Vibr-o-sonic buzzing away like a bumblebee.

Just wait till Mom gets home, will there be trouble, I thought.

And there was!

Of course, I didn't mention the Vibr-o-sonic to Mom, because what she didn't have to know about, she didn't have to know about, did she? I hid that in the back of my cupboard.

But I told her John had been spying on me while I was changing and that he'd seen me naked and that he watched and watched and wouldn't go away. Well, it was true in a way; he must have watched for at least twenty minutes!

My God, did Mom go mad!

"You want me to call the police, John? It's against the law to spy on a female, and especially the young madam."

"I didn't look, Madam!"

"He did, Mom, truly!"

"No, Madam, I was just filling the watering can to wash

the car. The tap is by that window. I didn't look inside, Madam."

"He did, Mom; he's lying!"

"Well, John, what have you got to say for yourself? I think we must call the police."

"No, Madam. I was filling the watering can. And I was hearing the *bzzz, bzzz,* and I just look to see if the machine is on."

"What machine?" Mom asked.

"Madam, I don't know. Maybe it's the radio still on."

"Was the radio on, Ruthie?" Mom asked.

"No, Mom, he's not telling the truth. He looked through that window a long time."

"John, I've had enough. I think it's better to call the police. You can tell them about the watering can and the radio. See if they believe you."

"No, Madam, please. Don't call the police."

"I work for lawyers, you know. They can take you to the courts and have you in jail for this. It is a big offense. It's the Act of Immorality," Mom said. "African people can spend many years in jail for this crime."

"No, Madam. I didn't do it."

"Are you calling Ruthie a liar?"

"No, Madam. I was looking to see the noise, Madam."

"Go to your room now, John," Mom said. "I'll think about what to do. Maybe I'll phone the police . . ."

"No, Madam, please . . ."

". . . and they'll come and take you away . . ."

"No, Madam, please . . ."

John was begging like a young piccanin.

". . . but anyway, you'll be finished working here . . ."

"No, Madam, I like working for the madam. I didn't do it, Madam."

John skulked off to his room, and Mom took me into the breakfast room to talk.

"That frightened him," Mom said.

"Aren't you going to call the police?" I asked her.

"Do you really want this thing to be discussed by other people, Ruthie? You'll be the one who gets the bad reputation."

"So what are you going to do?"

"Get rid of him, but first just let him think about the police for a while, so that he leaves without any trouble."

When Mannie heard that John was going to be fired, he hit the roof.

"You'll never get such a good boy again!" he shouted. Who would've ever thought Mannie would call John "a good boy"? "It will take months to teach another boy all the chores." Obviously Mannie was concerned about how long it would take another boy to learn how to bring a mango into the bathroom. "What's he done that's so wrong?"

When Mom told him, Mannie said something I'll never forget.

"She probably provoked him!"

When I heard him say that I went mad. The pressure in my head was too much. I took a step toward the sideboard, and in a couple of wild movements, screaming as I did it, I knocked all Mannie's trash African figurines on to the floor. They went flying, shattering into bits.

Mannie was furious and tried to grab hold of me, but I picked up his ivory ornament and held it above my head.

It was heavy and would have crushed Mannie's face if he took one step nearer to me.

He didn't. He stepped back, turned to my mom and said, "She's mad. She'll kill someone one of these days."

6

The next few days were grim. I was in a real state. My head was so confused. I was cross with everyone: Mannie, because of what he'd said to me; Mom, because she still kept Mannie on in the house; Lenore, because she blamed me for upsetting Mom; the garden boy John, for spying on me; and myself, maybe most of all, for being such a messed-up person.

I couldn't even look at Mannie after that incident, and he couldn't stand the sight of me either. Mom wasn't speaking to him. She said she could never forgive him for what he said about me.

Mom was worried about me, too, I could tell. But she didn't say anything to me. This incident was too much. It was the straw that broke the camel's back and made her wonder if I was as innocent as I claimed. I think it was the first time she ever realized that I was seventeen, with a whole bundle of my own emotions and desires. But she found it difficult to talk about these things.

7

Mom fired John the day he spied on me, as she said she would. She told him she'd give him half an hour to leave.

He moaned all the time while he hurriedly packed a few belongings, and he protested his innocence until he was outside the gate. But threatened with the police, he had no choice.

Emily was terribly upset. She stood in a corner of the kitchen and would hardly speak to anyone. She just shook her head and said "Tch! Tch! Tch!" Nobody could tell if she was agitated because John had done such a thing, or because he was having to leave.

He stood outside the house for half an hour, perhaps in the hope that we might change our minds and call him back. But he finally got the picture, and when we peeped out from the lounge curtains, he looked daggers at us and walked off down Noreen Avenue, scowling.

When he had gone, Mom went in to check his room. She found it was all smoky and eventually found this metal lid of a jar that had stuff in it that was still smoking. It hadn't been used as an ashtray; it was more like something had been burnt in that lid.

Mom showed it to me before she threw it away to prove to me that John was a dagga addict.

But when I looked in that lid, all I could see was a few burnt leaves and something that looked like burnt slivers . eggshell. In a corner of the room I noticed a shoe box half-full of leaves, small bones, feathers, and seashells.

But it was Mom who found the snake.

She screamed when she saw it, curled in the bottom drawer of the small cupboard.

It was dead, of course—dried out.

But it still looked awesome.

There was no mistaking it as a puff adder.

I asked Emily later if she knew why John had kept a dead puff adder in his room.

She hesitated, but then decided to tell me.

"You know when he cut his arms, Rootie. He take out the poison from the snake's teeth. And he mix it with some chopped-up leaves and some other things. And he push the poison in the cuts."

"What for?" I asked her.

"He was too frightened Isaac will kill him. This *muti* makes him strong. Nobody can kill him now."

8

The new boy, Joseph, was about sixty years old and a bit deaf. Mom thought he wouldn't give me any trouble because he was long past visiting shebeens and spying on white girls and that sort of thing.

Mannie wasn't satisfied with Joseph. He found fault with everything he did.

"He's not as good as John," Mannie kept saying.

From the way he spoke so well of John, you'd have thought they had been the best of friends. Whereas the truth was a million miles away.

About a week after John had left, I locked myself in my

bedroom, put a piece of cardboard behind the damaged venetian blind, and got out the Vibr-o-sonic Massager. I tried to put the shiny image of John's black face out of my mind as I lay there and prayed for the machine to do its work.

Every day for two weeks I tried, and Joseph worked in the garden all that time. I had no botheration from him at all.

Nearly every day I measured myself. And sometimes when I looked in the mirror, I thought I could see big improvements. But the tape measure never lied. In two weeks that Vibr-o-sonic added exactly no inches to my bust. Not even a fraction of one inch. I was at my wits' end. I thought of sending it back with a nasty note about cheating the public, but then in the instruction booklet I reread the letters from satisfied customers whose breasts had grown by anything from one inch to seven inches, in the case of Miss Annetjie du Toit, of Stellenbosch, whose picture I greatly envied. She must have used the Vibr-o-sonic twenty-four hours a day to get like that. I would have had to abscond from school forever in order to use that machine so much, and I didn't think that was a very good idea in my matriculation year, not with the exams looming up in November.

That Vibr-o-sonic was my last hope. I mean, your body isn't going to wake up suddenly aged seventeen and say "Hey! Isn't it time we started adding a bit of flesh here and a bit of flesh there? This girl's getting a bit depressed about being too flat here and too flat there."

Larry waited and waited and waited, until his itchy fingers were cramped with the waiting. Between his anxiety and my anxiety I began to understand how a person could even resort to nose ops and silicone implants, and I was thinking of making inquiries myself. But I didn't know who to ask. The only person I knew who was an expert on such subjects was Mr. Malamud, but no way would I ever have approached him.

Nevertheless, the electricity between Larry and me was still high-voltage, and I fancied him like mad. I loved driving at his side in the Austin Healey and going with him to parties and films.

If it wasn't for the anxiety that tightened my stomach, I could even have believed that Larry was very fond of me, too.

9

The simmering anger between Mannie and Mom erupted one night into a massive argument.

It started when Mannie came storming into the breakfast room.

"We must get a new boy!" he shouted. His voice was so loud I'm sure Joseph could easily have heard every word from the backyard. "This one is too old. And he forgets everything I tell him. Today he spilled coffee on my Vaal Reef dividends report."

"He will learn," Mom answered. "Give him time."

"He's too old to be useful," Mannie shouted.

"You'll soon be that age," Mom said. "Anyway, he's good with the garden."

"But he doesn't even know which way to put the knives and forks."

"You must teach him slowly."

"I do. Every day. But still he puts them back-to-front. And he looks stupid when he serves us."

"Mannie, what are you hucking me for? Leave me alone!"

"Are we not going to speak again?" he asked.

"Not until you apologize for what you said."

"Me apologize? What about Ruth? She broke all my statues."

Mannie had tried to glue back the broken bits of his figurines, but he'd done a lousy job. The hands looked deformed, and all the spears and drums and mortars and pestles were now crooked in their owners' arms.

"Is that all you can think of, those rubbish statues? I don't even like them in my house."

"*Your* house?" Mannie shrieked. "I thought we shared this house."

Well, that made Mom hit the roof.

"You come live in my house, you don't contribute a bladdy cent, you lie around all day in your dressing gown, you insult Ruth. . . ."

I could hear it all from my room. Good for you, Mom, I thought. It was time she had all this out with him.

"You don't like the way I behave?" Mannie screamed. "You're just a nervous wreck yourself! What do you ever give me? You don't give me love. What kind of a woman are you?"

"What are you saying?" Mom screamed. "Bertha was right about you."

Mom was getting hysterical; I could tell from her voice.

"That bladdy Bertha turned you against me from the start."

"But she's right. You tormented your first wife just like you're tormenting me."

"How dare you mention my wife!" Mannie screamed.

It was getting vicious in there. I thought of going in to protect Mom if Mannie turned on her.

Then Mom screamed. No words, just a scream. I thought, my God, this time he's hit her, the bastard.

I ran into the passage and so did Lenore. We ran down to their bedroom—the door was closed.

"Mom, are you all right?" I shouted.

"Go away!" Mannie shouted. "It's none of your business!"

"Mom, are you all right?" I shouted again.

"It's all right, Ruthie," Mom sobbed. Her voice was convulsed with pain.

Lenore looked at me. I couldn't work out what her eyes were saying. Was she cross with me? Lenore didn't say anything. She was always so clammed up when you most wanted to hear what she was feeling.

I went back to my room. There was no more screaming, just soft voices and talking.

Later, Mom came out of the room with these dark-purple rings around her eyes because she'd been sobbing so much. She went to the kitchen and made herself an Ovaltine.

"Are you all right, Mom?" I asked her, feeling very tender toward her.

"Yes, but he's a swine, that man."

"I told you that he was," I said, but she interrupted me.

"I don't want to talk now, Ruthie," she said. "I don't feel too marvelous."

Later that evening, Mom collapsed in the toilet.

Mannie called Dr. Glass, and he told her she needed rest. Her blood pressure wasn't right, and for the sake of her health, she should relax more.

Mannie assured Dr. Glass that he would take care of Mom. He held Mom's hand as she lay there in the bed, and he looked so upset. She did look awful—her eyes had sunk into the bony hollows of her head. Her skin was pale, almost yellow.

The doc said that she should take time off work and have a nice holiday, maybe at the Wigwam in Rustenberg, or somewhere peaceful, with lots of fresh air.

But Mannie said he'd just had a holiday in Durban, and anyway, he didn't like mountains, but not to worry, he'd make sure she relaxed at home just as if she were on holiday in the peaceful mountains. And Dr. Glass seemed to believe his every word.

10

After Mom's blackout, Mannie was kind to her, I must admit. He let Mom sleep and brought her breakfast in bed; he wouldn't let her take any phone calls, and he insisted that she took two weeks off work. When she had regained some of her strength, he even drove to the library in her new Zephyr 6 and borrowed two books for her to read. And he drove to Crystal's and bought her a cheesecake, which was her favorite. In fact, he liked driving that Zephyr 6 so much that I thought his next kindness might extend to driving all the way down to Cape Town to bring her back some seawater in a bottle.

Mom took a few days to get back on her feet, but Mannie was reluctant to concede that she was getting better.

"Another day in bed won't do you any harm," he said tenderly. "I'll bring you breakfast again tomorrow."

He was so considerate to Mom that I began to wonder if I understood their relationship after all. Maybe that's why Mom never chucked him out the house.

Every day he drove somewhere or other for her. But after a while Mom started running around the house like she was training for the marathon, just to prove to him how much better she was. In the end she had to fight to get back the use of her own car. And she got quite worked up about it. It happened one day when she wanted to go to the supermarket.

"OK, if you feel better," Mannie said. "But at least let me drive you there. There's a lot of tension in driving."

"There's a lot of tension for me when you drive," Mom said, which was true, because Mannie was the most erratic driver. He had this style of cruising along too slowly and then accelerating at unusual moments, which was enough to give Mom the schluck.

"I'm only trying to be helpful," Mannie whined.

"Then I'll drive and you help me in the supermarket," Mom said, wrenching the keys from Mannie.

"You don't have to use force," Mannie shouted. "I would have given them to you if you asked."

The hollows of her eyes still had a purple tinge, and I thought it did her no good to be shouting and fighting over car keys.

"Now I'm not coming with you to the supermarket."
Mannie sulked. He was very mature about such things.

So much for Mom having a peaceful mountain holiday
in her very own home.

11

Two weeks later, Mom was back at work, and Mannie was
his old self again.

There was trouble at his business. A huge property deal
was going wrong. A company who had shown interest in a
building plot in the center of Joburg were now favoring a
new site at the opposite end of town for their multistory
shopping complex. Mannie blamed Ullman, and from what
we could gather, Ullman blamed Mannie for never being
there.

The net result was that Mannie was in a bad mood.

"It's going to be one of the biggest shopping centers in
Africa, and Ullman is buggering up the deal! Can you believe it?"

Mannie was so upset, he had difficulty falling asleep at
night. Mom told him if he didn't sleep during the day he'd
sleep better at nights. But he wouldn't hear of it, and he was
up half the night, restlessly moving from room to room, not
knowing what to do with himself. Invariably he'd go back to
his bedroom at some unearthly hour and wake Mom, with no
consideration for the fact that she had a full day's work ahead
of her. Then he'd keep her up half the night. Of course, the
next day the sock would be on his bedroom handle all day.

Mom had always slept in the bed that was nearer the door, but she got so annoyed with the way he woke her at nights that she insisted on swapping the positions of their beds. She got Joseph to move Mannie's bed nearer to the door, and her one to where Mannie's used to be, on the far side of the room, next to the wall. That way, she thought, she would have some chance of sleeping through Mannie's restlessness, while he could go in and out of the room without disturbing her.

The business deal finally fell through. Mannie's sleep pattern worsened to the point where he was going through anguish at nights. Mom told him to go to a doctor for sleeping tablets, and that's what set him off.

"I don't need sleeping tablets!" he said, loud enough for both Lenore and I to hear, in our separate bedrooms. "I need a proper wife in bed."

That was the first time I heard that Mom was withholding her favors from him.

Next time I was alone with Mom after Mannie had gone to sleep, I asked her why she didn't ask him to leave.

"I can't," she said. "Where would he go? I'm all he's got now."

"But you don't love him."

"Stop it, Ruth!"

"You know he's selfish."

"Yes, but . . ."

"Come on, Mom, he keeps you up all night. Look at you! You look a hundred years old."

"Thank you, Ruth. You say such nice things."

"Admit it once and for all, Mom. You can't stand him! At nights you don't even let him . . ."

I never finished the sentence. Mannie had come into the room. Obviously he couldn't sleep and had heard every word I'd been saying.

"So, now we see you in your true colors. You're the one poisoning your mom against me." He went and stood near Mom and put his arm around her shoulders. "Your mom and me are married, and we're going to stay that way," he said quietly. "There's nothing you can ever do about that. If you don't like it, you can leave."

"Don't talk that way, Mannie," Mom said, but she didn't shake off his arm or anything.

"You are a spoiled little girl," he said to me. "Your mother gives you everything, but still you torment her. It's you! Can't you see that? Lenore doesn't cause any trouble. She and I get on perfectly well together. But you've got a vicious little mind. You've never accepted me."

I wanted to say something that would knock him flat, that would deflate his fat paunch and leave him writhing in his selfishness. But the words wouldn't come.

He squeezed Mom toward his paunch and asked her to come to bed. His performance made me livid.

"Let's go to sleep," he said to her. "You look tired, my dear."

12

I rang the bell of Bobby's place in Parktown, even though the front door was open.

A middle-aged lady, looking something like a gypsy with long skirt and headband, opened the door.

She told me I could come in and wait for Bobby in his room.

I carried my suitcase to his room, sat down on his bed, and wondered what he'd say when he saw me.

I suppose I could have gone to Barney and Helen, but Bobby had said I should come over if I ever needed space for my head. I reckoned I needed that space now more than ever. The money for rent was a problem, but I'd sort that out when I came to it.

Bobby came home late and found me asleep.

He gave me a coffee, and we chatted for hours. He told me there was a room free in the house for a week or two, while Ginger was on holiday, but he didn't sound too keen on my staying. I thought maybe it was because I wasn't friends with Alan anymore. After all, why should he do me a favor?

"It's not the rent," he said. "You can stay for a couple of weeks without paying rent. But you're still at school. . . ."

"Only for another four months," I said.

"Even so, your mother will want you home, and you've got your matric to finish, and all that. If you were an independent person, it would be a different story."

"But how can I get to be an independent person if I don't move away from home?"

"It will happen," he said. "Listen, you're exhausted; we'll talk some more tomorrow."

I liked it in Ginger's room, even though I knew it couldn't last. There was a stone Buddha in one corner of his room with an expression that I at first thought was indifference. But each day its expression warmed up, and I even began to see it as a serene smile.

I phoned Mom every day so that she wouldn't panic, but I never told her where I was. Those phone calls were traumatic, I can tell you, and I learned a way of saying the minimum without being hurtful.

I phoned Larry the first day, but not again. I needed a rest, to see how I really felt about everything.

Bobby was out most of the time, involved with student politics at the university, so I didn't see that much of him. But when he came back, he often looked in on me. Sometimes he had Dawn with him. She was concerned about me in a quiet way.

"Aren't you bothered about missing school?" she asked me.

"Not really," I said.

"You should take advantage of education," she said. "There's plenty of people your age in this country being offered next to nothing."

I shrugged my shoulders.

"You should think about it, Ruth," Bobby said. "You could make something of your life if you pull yourself together."

I had the feeling Bobby was losing patience with me. He didn't seem as tolerant of me as on past occasions. I thought maybe he was studying too hard, or perhaps he had reasons for not wanting me to stay.

It was a house with a tremendous amount of activity. There were always people coming in and out of it, so that it was difficult to work out who actually lived there. I knew Greg lived there, the bearded chap I had met the time I'd visited with Alan. And Sonia, the gypsy lady, who was, in fact, a teacher. Of course, Bobby lived there, and Ginger, who I'd never met but was studying philosophy, judging by the books in his room. There were also a couple of musicians, because every now and again, day or night, music would break out from one or another room and would sometimes go on for several hours. Then there was the couple—I don't know if they were married or just living together—who lived in what used to be the servants' quarters. And there was Anne, who wrote poetry.

I'd say in total there were about nine or ten people living there. That's not counting Patrick, the African man who lived in the Pump Room, an old brick shed, half-filled with useless, rusting machinery. The other half of the room was taken up with his paintings, mostly richly colored pastels of birds and Africans fused together into one body.

I didn't socialize much, I suppose because I wasn't permanent. But everyone was friendly toward me. At least they treated me like a real person.

One night Ben popped in to see me.

He knocked on the door, and when I opened it, he took my hand with his slapping handshake and said, "Ruth, howzit going? I didn't expect to find you here. Where's the reluctant doctor?"

I wondered who he meant for a minute, then I realized he meant Alan.

"I don't know," I said. "I haven't seen him for ages. I'm staying here for a few days."

"Yes, I know. Bobby told me about your circumstances."

We talked a lot. I discovered that he was very intelligent and had a degree in politics and English. He worked at Juta's Bookshop in the storeroom, though he had never mentioned his degree to his employers.

"Otherwise I couldn't keep the job," he told me. "So I

pretend to be stupid. 'Yes, my baas, no my baas, whatever you say, my baas.' They think I go home to Alexandra Township every night and eat my mielie-pap. They don't even know that I use their lending library."

He showed me one of the books he had "borrowed" to read in his spare time.

"Listen to this," he said, opening the book and reading from it.

It shocked me, I must admit. Somehow it was even worse hearing it read by a nonwhite person.

The passages he read argued that the white man must reduce every other race to servitude, because the divinity of the white skin was an ancient, biological fact. Primitive black people should never be allowed to deprive the whites of such a splendid land as South Africa. In fact, the so-called liberation of subpeoples should never be allowed, and exponents of liberalism should be liquidated.

"What do you think of that?" Ben asked.

"I've never heard anything so horrible," I said.

"There's eleven thousand books banned in this country," Ben said, "because they could provoke trouble, but this one is not banned. Now, there's logic for you. In fact, the South African Broadcasting Corporation thinks this book is marvelous. It calls it a clarion call for the republic. I'm writing a review of it in my spare time for the *Rand Daily Mail*." He suddenly broke into a smile. "Hey, let's not only talk politics," he said. "How long are you going to be staying here?"

13

On the Saturday night a lot of people turned up, and pretty soon a party was under way with music and enormous amounts of drink. There were quite a few black people, including Patrick from the Lodge, mingling with the white people as though it were not immoral, which of course it wasn't, except in the government's eyes. One thing I noticed was that the black men were less interested in the black girls than they were in the white girls. And Anne, the poet—or poetess, I suppose I should say—was more interested in black men than she was in white men. In fact, the longer the evening went on, the more interested she seemed to get.

I mingled with Bobby and Dawn mostly, though I don't suppose they wanted me hanging around them. They were like two lovebirds taking an evening off study and politics to be together. It was so obvious they enjoyed each other's company. But they were good to me and introduced me to a lot of the guests. They seemed very comfortable in that mixed-race gathering.

Later in the night, I recognized a face across the room. It was Ben. He came over to me with a broad smile on his face.

"Howzit, Ruth! Let's dance, hey?"

Before my mind could really think of an objection, he had taken hold of my hand and begun to move with the music. I think it would have been awkward for me to dance with any other African bloke, but Ben was so easy-going and friendly, it would have been rude of me to refuse.

I was very nervous, and my stomach felt distinctly uncomfortable. Actually, it was worse than that. I was afraid.

Afraid of what? I didn't know. Afraid of crossing so many boundaries all at once, I suppose.

Ben sensed my feelings, I'm sure of it, because when the music ended he thanked me and went across to some people he knew.

I saw him at various moments during the night, laughing and dancing with other white girls, all of them older than I was. I wished I had been able to be as relaxed with him.

Later, he bumped into me when I was helping myself to some cocktail sausages.

"Have you ever seen so many liberal whites in one room together?" he asked me. "And liberal blacks!" he added, smiling. "You've got to be a damn liberal black to mix with whites, you know."

I couldn't help laughing.

"So, are you enjoying yourself?" he asked. "Don't you like dancing?"

"No, I do, but I don't know anyone," I said clumsily.

"You know *me*," he said, taking my hand. "Let's have another go, what do you say?"

It was a slow dance. Ben started off holding me at arm's length, but after a while he pulled me toward him and our bodies made contact. I could feel the tension in my own body as I tried to hold back, without making it noticeable.

Ben didn't insist. He let me dance at a comfortable distance, and he made pleasant conversation with me. But when the music stopped he again excused himself and went back to his other friends.

I turned to talk to Sonia, who was sparkling with beads and bracelets, and I wondered if she dressed like this when she taught at school. She drank nonstop and told me the party would only liven up at midnight.

But at midnight I called it quits and went to my room. I knew I didn't belong there. It was deep water, and I could hardly swim.

Two days later, Uncle Barney turned up.

"How did you know where I was?"

"We've known for a while. Your mom has been phoning everyone, she's so worried. Won't you consider going home?"

14

Little Hymie was being seen by a psychologist five afternoons a week. Sometimes they sat in the garden. This lady was trying to teach him to speak.

"Hymie, say b . . . b . . . b . . ."

Hymie looked up at the sky, turned his neck to try and look over his back, and then punched himself in the head.

"Say b . . . b . . . b . . ."

Hymie tried to scratch one of his facial scabs. I noticed Betty watching him from the back of the house.

"Hymie," the lady said, waving her hand in front of his eyes, "look here! B . . . b . . . b . . ."

Hymie let out one of his prehistoric groans, then suddenly stopped short and made a "b" sound. The lady popped a Smartie into his mouth as quick as lightning.

"Good, Hymie! Good!"

She stroked his face. Hymie almost smiled as if he were enjoying it, but a punch to his head followed immediately, so it was difficult to tell.

"Hymie, look here! T . . . t . . . t . . ."

The lady was persistent, I'll give her that much, but my feeling was that Hymie was beyond reach.

15

In Mom's book about the tribes of South Africa the picture of the python dance showed girls stomping in unison one behind the other, their almost naked bodies gleaming. With elbows bent, each girl held the arms of the girl in front of her, so that viewed from the sides, the long, writhing row of overlapping arms resembled a long, fat snake.

This was the famous python dance—part of the ritual initiation of Venda girls when they reached puberty.

After menstruation, Venda girls begin their initiation. They are taught about sexual behavior, betrothal, and marriage, and they are warned that just as a decaying carcass attracts cockroaches and flies, so disreputable girls attract undesirable suitors.

At a later stage, the girls are isolated in a large hut and given detailed instruction in childbearing and parenthood. They are also examined to check they are still virgins. Then they learn the intricate python dance, winding and unwinding around the fire, to the accompaniment of ceremonial drums, each girl wearing only a tiny apron across her loins.

The book also explained that a python always swallows its prey whole. When it does, it resembles a woman who is pregnant, containing a whole animal within herself. The only difference is that the python never gives birth to the animal it has swallowed. Instead, according to the Venda, the python gives birth to invisible spirits. To dream of a python before marriage is favorable because it indicates that there will be numerous and healthy offspring.

The picture showed thirty-eight girls—possibly thirty-nine, it's not all that clear—and each of them with firm, pouting breasts, just like Mannie's figurines. Not one of them was smaller than me!

It's lucky I wasn't born Venda, because no way would anyone ever have compelled me to appear naked like that with thirty-eight more well-endowed girls. It would have been absolutely humiliating!

But it did occur to me that white girls in Joburg could have done with some instruction in sexual behavior, marriage, and that sort of thing, just to prepare them better for life.

16

Larry wasn't pleased that I had staved him off for two weeks.

"There's plenty girls who would want to come out with me," he said, when I saw him.

"So why don't you go out with them then?"

"Because it's you I like," he said, welcoming me back into his arms. "Even though you're so stubborn."

I told him I had missed him terribly, but I'd needed the time to think things over.

"And what conclusions have you reached?"

"Just that I want to go out with you again," I said.

"You missed a slap-up party at Alwyn's place," he told me.

"Did I?"

"Yes, it turned into quite an orgy."

He proceeded to tell me the details, and my only feeling was relief. Thank heavens I'd been at Bobby's place, where I had the space to be myself.

"And did you participate?" I asked.

"What do you think, Ruth?"

"I don't know. Who did you go there with?"

"Libby."

Libby! I could just imagine what she and Larry had got up to!

17

On Saturday morning I went with Mom to the supermarket. I wanted to save her some of the strain of shopping. I suppose it was also my way of trying to make up for my little holiday from home.

In Norwood these piccanins came hopping between the cars as usual trying to sell us the *Star*. Mom didn't buy one, because it was delivered to our house every night, so

I didn't see the front page until I got home. I hardly ever read the newspaper, but that day before supper I was too lazy to do homework, so I just took a brief glance at the front page. Then I got a shock.

It was in this one article that mentioned the name Robert Gerber. My God, I thought, could he be related to Alan Gerber? The headline said "Wits Student Detained," and the article was all about this man Robert Gerber who was a member of the Students' Representative Council. Apparently he went to Basutoland for subversive reasons and was a member of the South African Communist Party, and had some connection with this banned lawyer called Gerrit Viljoen, who even I had heard of. The article went on to say that Gerber was finally caught painting slogans on a bridge somewhere in Roodepoort of all places. It also mentioned another man who was arrested with Mr. Gerber by the name of Benjamin Dhlamini, but it didn't say much about this man, except that he was found with incriminating documents on his person.

By the time I was finished reading this article, I could feel a kind of trembling in my bones, as if there was an earth tremor happening somewhere very close, with its epicenter under my very own feet.

Robert Gerber?

Then it dawned on me.

It was Bobby! The police had arrested Bobby. Detained him without trial.

I couldn't believe it. This surely couldn't be happening to someone I knew. And Ben also, by the sound of it. I didn't have a clue what Ben's surname was, but Dhlamini sounded as good as any.

Oh my God!

PART SIX

1

I WALKED TO MY ROOM IN A DAZE. I WANTED
to phone Alan to see if it was true. But I hadn't spoken to
him for so long that it would have seemed impolite to
phone him suddenly out of the blue.

I thought of talking to Mom about it, but I knew how
frightened she was of politics.

It was Larry I asked in the end. After all, he was a law
student.

"Have you heard of Robert Gerber?" I asked.

"He's that commie who's been detained, isn't he?"

"What's going to happen to him?" I asked.

"I don't know the whole case," he answered. "But he
was involved with Gerrit Viljoen, so he's probably in big
trouble. Why do you ask?"

"Because he's Alan's brother. I know him."

"Really?" Larry said. "I didn't know you ever hung around with communists."

"I didn't know he was one," I said. "He's a really nice guy, I can tell you that. Do you know anything about Gerrit Viljoen?"

"Only that he's wanted for planning acts of sabotage. He gave the police the slip months ago, and he's been in hiding from them ever since."

Larry was keen to see *Alphaville* at the Victory, but I wasn't in the mood for a film about space. I had enough trouble trying to live on this planet, the way things were going. But in the end I went, and the only thing in that film I liked was the girl who didn't know about love on her planet. The word "love" wasn't in her dictionary.

"What will they do to Bobby Gerber?" I asked Larry on the way home.

"Have you been thinking of him right through the film?" he asked. "They'll probably beat the hell out of him until they get an admission of guilt."

"Can't something be done for him?"

"I don't know," Larry said, and he dropped me off moodily at home and zoomed off in the Austin Healey.

2

The next day Mom went back to work, and by the time she came home I was a bag of nerves.

It all came out in the breakfast room that night.

"Zlotkin's got this case involving the ritual murder of a

man. Can you believe it? They killed him, and then they ate the man's insides . . ."

"Mom, I can't bear it tonight. Do you have to talk about these things?" I said.

"What's wrong with you?" she said.

"I'm very upset, that's what," I said.

"What about?" she asked.

"About Alan's brother," I said, and I told her about him being in prison and all that.

"Well, there's nothing you can do about it," she said. "And you've got your matric exams coming soon. You've already missed too much school this year because of your escapades. You can't get involved in politics. It's danger-ous."

"You're always saying that," I said. "How can you just stand by and watch everything happening? Besides, I know Bobby Gerber, and that makes it different. He's a friend, and he let me stay at his place."

I didn't dare tell her that I also knew Ben Dhlamini and, what's more, that I'd even danced with him.

"You don't owe the Gerbers anything," Mom said. "You don't even see Alan anymore. I always knew that family wasn't any good."

"Mom, you're really something, you know," I said, walking out of the room.

3

A week after I heard the news about Bobby and Ben being arrested, I was still feeling awful. I was getting on every-

one's nerves, and likewise, everyone was getting on my
nerves. It was just like the advert said: Where's the easy-
going and likeable part of you gone? Your nerves are hungry for Sanatogen.

But I knew it wasn't Sanatogen I needed. It was to speak
to Alan. Eventually I plucked up courage and phoned him.
His voice sounded dead.

"I can't speak on the phone," he said.

"Are you all right, Alan?"

"It's not me we have to worry about," he said.

"I know that. It's Bobby . . ."

It was awful trying to get the right words out.

"I told you we can't speak on the phone about that."

"Can I come over and speak to you, Alan?"

My God, I've never had such a difficult conversation
with anyone. And it wasn't that much easier when I went
to his house.

For a start, Mr. Gerber had aged terribly. His hair had
literally gone grey. I couldn't believe a physical change
could happen that quickly. He looked like one of these
people in a film who have seen a real ghost, or a werewolf
has come into their living room and really frightened the
pants off them.

"Ruth, we haven't seen you for a long time," he said,
putting his arm affectionately around me and then remain-
ing silent for a split second before letting me go again.

"It's terrible about Bobby, Mr. Gerber," I said, not
knowing what to say, but thinking I ought to say something.

He couldn't answer me. I'm sure he was overcome with
worry.

The house was very quiet. Donnay and little Sam were

sitting on the lounge floor doing a puzzle of Peter Pan and Captain Hook. They said hello to me, but that's all, as if they had been told to be quiet so much that they were afraid to move. To me they seemed like punctured balloons sitting there.

Mrs. Gerber was trying to look brave, but when she hugged me, tears came into her eyes.

"He's done nothing wrong. He's still my baby boy," she said. And then she added, "Thank you for coming to see us, Ruth. It's so lovely to see you again."

I hadn't even realized that I had come to see the Gerber family, but now that I was there I was pleased I had.

"A lot of our friends are too frightened to come now," she said. "But Alan will be so happy you're here. He's taken it very badly, you know."

She could have said that again. Alan looked like he hadn't shaved for about a week, and the same went for washing as well—he had this sort of stink coming off him. Maybe he just hadn't changed his clothes for a week.

We went into his room.

4

Bobby had been taken into an interrogation room where he was made to stand on a brick.

For hours and hours he stood on that brick, and each time he stepped off it, he was punched and verbally abused. He hardly knew if it was day or night. The room was lit by a bare light bulb hanging over his head.

Geldenhuys, the interrogator, asked him endless questions, beating him across the face whenever he thought Bobby lied, until Bobby's mouth was cut and bleeding in several places.

Several times Bobby blanked out, falling asleep on his feet, only to be woken by a punch in the stomach or a blow across the face.

When he was at the limit of his endurance, Geldenhuys left the room and Venter came in.

"That Geldenhuys is a bastard," he said. "Here, have a drink of water. Now, if you just tell me all we need to know, then you can go back home to your family and friends."

Venter stayed for a few hours, until Geldenhuys returned—more ferocious than ever.

"Get out of here, Venter! You're too soft on this chap. We must kick the shit out of him so that he tells us the truth."

And so Bobby was brutally assaulted again and again, his face and ribs severely bruised and cut, and he was never allowed to move off his brick or to sleep.

"We've got your girlfriend, what's her name, Dawn, in the next cell, and I'm warning you, if you don't speak soon, we're going to fuck her. First Venter will fuck her, then me."

On and on, relentlessly, for four days, until Bobby was hallucinating with pain and lack of sleep.

5

We were silent for a while. I couldn't think of one thing to say. Everything seemed so meaningless, all of a sudden.

"We didn't even know where he was the first few days," Alan said. "He just disappeared from an economics lecture. Two plainclothes men came and took him away. Nobody knew about it. They didn't notify us or anything. For all we knew, he had been killed somewhere, and that's why he wasn't at his flat. In the end my father made inquiries and found out he was in Pretoria Prison. And Ben is in there too."

"That's terrible," I said.

"Yes, and because Ben's an African, they're probably doing even worse things to him. Nobody has heard."

Worse things? What worse things? And why? Because his skin was black? Why would anyone want to do such things to him?

I couldn't say anything. I couldn't keep saying "That's terrible" or something like that. My eyes were too dry even to cry. So I just sat and listened. And Alan spoke when he felt like it.

"Can you imagine what it's like for them?" he asked me.

"It must be terrible," I said.

I wanted to ask if they had stopped torturing Bobby, but I didn't know how to ask that question without sounding stupid.

"I can't sleep at night now myself," he said. "I just keep imagining Bobby in that prison."

I wanted to put my arm around Alan, to give him some comfort. But then, how could I comfort him? My bit of comforting couldn't even get anywhere near the pain he was going through.

"Now he's in solitary," Alan said. "With just a Bible. That's all they allow him to read. And no real visitors."

"Oh God!" I said. "How can they do things like that to human beings?"

When I got home, I went to my room and had a long cry. I couldn't bear to think of what was being done to Bobby and Ben. And Alan had looked so forlorn and despairing. It had been impossible to talk like we used to. The openness was gone. I suppose a lot of that was because I had given him the brush-off, and maybe he wasn't even that keen on me coming to see him. Still, I felt better somehow for going, even though I didn't find out what Bobby and Ben had done to get themselves detained.

6

A week later Alan phoned me.

"You know when you were leaving," he said, "you asked if there was anything you can do?"

"Yes."

"Do you want to come to Wits University tonight? The students are having a protest demonstration."

"Yes, I'll come," I said.

Mom nearly hit the roof.

"You'll get in trouble, Ruth, I'm warning you. Don't say I didn't warn you! You're playing with fire. Those sort of students who protest, they're all communists, just like Robert Gerber. They'll all land up in prison sooner or later. Do you want to be among them?"

To tell the truth, I myself was frightened about the protest.

"Can't you understand, Mom? It's Bobby. He's been tortured, and he's been in solitary confinement for twenty days. I must do something to help."

"The police take photographs of everyone at those protests," Mannie said. "You'll be on police records if you go. Please don't go, Ruth."

Mannie actually seemed concerned about me—I couldn't believe it. And for once, he and Mom were in total agreement.

By the time Alan came to collect me, Mom was in a near-hysterical state of anxiety. But I had to go—the Gerbers were my friends. I left her standing on the stoep crying, with Mannie trying to comfort her.

Alan drove me to the university in the Borgward Isabella. He was eighteen now and had his driving license. The last time I'd been in that car, it was with Bobby driving and Ben in the backseat, joking about being a houseboy. But Bobby and Ben had no use for a car where they were.

There were about a hundred students and a few lecturers and professors at the protest. They lined Jan Smuts Avenue holding placards that said, "Free Robert Gerber!" and "Robert Gerber and Ben Dhlamini—Charge or Release!"

We stood among the protesters, some of whom were carrying torches with real flames burning, and we sang this one song over and over again:

We shall overcome,
we shall overcome,
we shall overcome some day,
because deep in my heart
I do believe
that we shall overcome some day.

Black and white together,
black and white together,
black and white together some day,
for deep in my heart
I do believe
that we shall overcome some day.

It was so moving. I had shivers going down my spine every time we sang this song. I felt that surely everyone driving past and hearing us must feel equally moved. But God, I couldn't have been more wrong! Quite a few people in cars screamed at us.

"Bladdy communists! Kaffirboeties! Kaffir lovers! Go home to Russia!"

And they used their hands to make obscene gestures at us. One bloke even threw a bottle which smashed on the pavement about fifteen feet from where we were standing.

But we went on singing until eleven o'clock that night. And it was the most wonderful sound I ever heard in my life. I was frightened, but also I felt so good to be there with everyone and to be doing something at last for Bobby and Ben.

7

On the way home, Alan said thanks for coming. I told him thanks for asking, and I would do it again.

I felt something like a breeze come across me for a moment, and I wondered if I could like him again. Maybe I just felt close to him because of the protest singing being so emotional. One thing though, he would have to shave and clean himself up if he wanted me to like him again.

"I've stopped going to lectures," he said.

"Have you given up medicine?" I asked.

"Yes, I can't be bothered with it anymore. I'm not meant to be a doctor."

"What are you going to do?"

"No idea. I can't think straight anymore."

8

It was true that something heavy was going on in his brain. When I went to the Gerbers the following Sunday, he took me into the lounge and played me Mahler's Tenth Symphony on the hi-fi system.

"Mahler died while he was writing this music," he said.

I listened to the great swirling sounds, ebbing and flowing like an ocean of feelings.

Suddenly, as the music reached a crescendo, Alan jumped up and switched off the system.

"I can't listen to those discords," he said. "It makes the blood drain out of my head. I feel faint."

He sat down and held his head between his hands.

"So much for cheating death, hey?"

"What do you mean?" I asked.

"Mahler was superstitious about ninth symphonies. He didn't number his ninth symphony because he was afraid he'd die after that, like so many other composers had. Then he wrote another symphony and thought he'd cheated death. But he died before he ever completed the tenth."

I wanted to go over and hold Alan. He looked so depressed and hurt, as if the world had let him down.

"The ninth symphony is a limit," he said. "You can't go beyond it. Maybe there's things about life we can never know."

"Alan, are you all right?" I asked him.

"Yes. I mean no, not really."

I went over to the armchair where he was sitting, and I held Alan's hand. His fingernails were not clean, and if there's one thing I couldn't stand it was filthy fingernails. But I held him in spite of those feelings because there were feelings deeper inside of me that were more important.

"Ruth, what's happening?"

9

By the middle of September it was confirmed that the drought was the worst in fifty years. Many rivers had dried up completely, and the Vaaldam had fallen below 28 percent of its capacity. On the Platteland, even ploughs were unable to penetrate the sun-beaten, brick-hard crust that was covering the land. Priests were calling for a day of prayer to ask God to send spring rains.

They were also saying that women's skirts should not be more than three inches above the knee, that slacks were immoral, and that bare midriffs should be banned.

It was a dry time all right.

10

The Gerbers' lawyer discovered that Bobby was in a pretty bad state. Apparently he was having these visions or something that there were plagues of frogs in his cell, and that the Pharaohs wouldn't leave him alone. So much for having the Bible as your only companion. Bobby had lost a lot of weight and was having difficulty keeping his spirits up.

Even worse was the information that had somehow been smuggled out of the prison about Ben. I couldn't stand to hear it.

He was being tortured with electric shocks to his toes and genitals.

Oh my God!

Electric shocks to his toes and genitals!

I winced in anguish.

"The bladdy bastards!" Alan said. "Somebody should put five thousand volts through Verwoerd and his henchmen who do the dirty work!"

I felt a terrible anger surging up inside me. It was uncontrollable. I wanted to scream and cry and fight and scratch out the eyes of whoever was responsible.

Alan went to protest meetings and demonstrations nearly every day, and I went along at least once a week. It drove Mom to despair.

"You are going to get yourself in big trouble, my girl!" she said to me every time, without fail.

Maybe she was right, but I had no choice.

There were articles about Robert Gerber and Ben Dhlamini in all the newspapers, and the demonstrations got a lot of news coverage. It was obvious that Bobby knew Gerrit Viljoen, the banned lawyer, but it wasn't clear that Bobby or Ben had been involved with Viljoen's activities. There were letters to the *Star* and the *Rand Daily Mail* and the *Sunday Times* demanding that Bobby and Ben be charged or released, but after six weeks it looked like they were going to be detained indefinitely without trial.

I didn't see much of Larry during that time, or rather, he didn't see much of me. It wasn't that he was against protest demonstrations, but he was peeved about my involvement with the Gerbers.

Even so, he came along one night, and I stood between Alan and him the whole night, and we all sang "We Shall Overcome" together. But none of us spoke to each other much. We just stood there, each having our own thoughts, and Larry went home separately in his Austin Healey. It was taken for granted that I would go home with Alan, but there again, Alan did live near me and Larry lived in Mountainview, so there was no point him going out of his way, was there?

11

Little Hymie sat in the middle of a room. He wasn't wearing a crash helmet. There were wires attached to his body. Several interrogators were punching him, dealing heavy blows to his body and his face. They asked for the electric current to be switched on. His body writhed for a few seconds in pain. Then a lady appeared. She said, "Say b . . . b . . . b . . ." as she poured a continuous stream of Smarties from one bowl to another. "Say b . . . b . . . b . . ." Hymie looked around him. The iron-barred windows were high in the wall and let in little light. He uttered his primeval groan. "Say b . . . b . . . b . . ." The lady ate a Smartie herself. "Mmmm! They're delicious. Don't you want one?" Hymie reached for the bowl. "No you don't! Not until you say b . . . b . . . b . . ." Hymie's eyes rolled up to the ceiling. Then he stood up, detached the wires from his body, and said, "B . . . b . . . b . . . bladdy bastards!" The lady ran over to Hymie and hugged him. She said, "Hymie, you spoke! You spoke, my little boy! Here, have as many Smarties as you want!" Hymie tipped over the bowl. The Smarties went flying in all directions. "I don't like Smarties," he said. He walked to his cell door and said to his interrogators, "I'm going home now; I've had enough!" He opened the iron door and walked out into bright sunshine.

I woke up. There were tears rolling down my cheeks. I felt elated.

12

One weekend the Gerber family went to visit their relations in Potchefstroom. Alan was invited, but he refused. Which left him alone in the house. Merv persuaded him to invite a few people over.

"Don't waste the opportunity," Merv said. "Just a few couples. And we can get some food and wine."

Alan wasn't too keen at first, but Merv persisted. It was good of him really to try and take Alan's mind off his problems.

"What do you think, Ruth?" Alan asked.

"Well, I'll only come if you shave and wash!"

So that night at least, Alan washed himself and put on clean clothes, but he didn't completely keep his promise about shaving. He still had quite a beard, but it had been trimmed, I'll grant that.

Steve didn't show up even though he was invited. Nor did Cyril. Nothing could take Cyril's mind off his homosexual pursuits these days, Alan said. I had by then heard from lots of people that he had started spending his time at the Johannesburg Station, and that wasn't because he had an interest in steam engines. No, that was where homosexual men used to meet.

The reason Steve didn't show up was because he didn't want to come to the Gerbers' house. I knew that, and Alan knew as well. As a matter of fact, since Bobby's arrest Steve had been keeping away from Alan as if he had a contagious disease.

There were about half a dozen couples there that night, and during the first part of the evening Alan and I were very sociable. We both got a bit tipsy on Tassheimer wine, but as there were no parents about, there was no need to hide anyone's tipsiness.

The second part of the evening Alan and I were less sociable: we disappeared upstairs into Alan's bedroom. As soon as Alan locked the door, he told me he had missed me terribly.

"I don't know how I'd have got through these last few weeks without you," he said.

He took me in his arms and kissed me, really passionately.

After the nice things he'd said, I found myself responding. It was probably the wine, but Alan seemed so vulnerable, yet so sincere.

He switched off the light, took me to the bed, with its python skin wrapped around the side, and lay with me there. The only light came from a streetlight through the flimsy curtains. We talked softly and kissed.

Then I felt him slowly unbuttoning my blouse.

I felt paralyzed.

When he reached my bra, he put his hand underneath.

My heart stopped beating.

I held my breath.

I knew the moment had come.

He gave no sign of shock.

He just kissed me gently. Then he unclasped my bra, and I was exposed to him. Admittedly it was dark, but even so, nobody had bribed Alan to say what he said next. He said, "You're lovely, Ruth."

I couldn't believe it!

He said I was lovely.

After all my years of panic! After all my heartaches and sufferings and phobias! After all the nightmares!

He wasn't disappointed at all. He didn't comment about me having small breasts or complain that I had deceived him by wearing falsies. Actually, he didn't even notice any of that. He just said, "You're lovely, Ruth." He actually liked what he could see, and what he felt.

I hugged him out of pure joy and even let myself think for a moment that the word *love* might be in my dictionary after all.

It was beautiful in that room with Alan. Even if he was a bit crazed about Bobby being locked up, and even though he was so intense about how much he cared for me, still I felt we got very close that night. We seemed to reach into each other's hearts, where feelings were so delicate, yet so real. We held on to each other as if we were meant for each other, to give each other this mutual support and encouragement and, perhaps, even love.

Alan was gentle with me. He seemed to appreciate me so much. He caressed me and whispered beautiful things to me, and probably we both got carried away. It was as if we had found a sanctuary from the awful events of the past weeks, and we wanted to enjoy that special place to the utmost.

Maybe it was because he was a bit crazed that I let it happen, and that it happened so easily. After all, a crazy bloke might not notice things that he might notice at other times. But on the other hand, maybe I let it happen because I felt sorry for him. No, that's not true either. I really had a good feeling about him, and that's all there was to it.

It was probably the relief from all my worries that made me throw caution to the wind. I suppose I wanted to make up for lost time, to find out what it was like to be a real woman.

13

The day after the party I disposed of the Vibr-o-sonic Breast Massager. I felt light as air. Alan liked me as I was. It was unreal. I kept my padded bras because obviously I couldn't walk around looking a quarter of the size I had previously been. I decided to reduce the size of the pads slowly over the next few months, and I started a diet to explain away why I would be getting slimmer. But did I feel pleased with the world—in that respect at least!

If Mom would have known what Alan and I had been up to, she would doubtless have had a nervous break-down—it was her worst nightmare come true. But she would never know, because who would tell her? Not me, that's for sure.

The Tuesday after Merv's get-together, Alan came round.

"Have you heard the news?"

"What is it?" I asked. "Have they been released?"

"No, unfortunately," he said. "Verwoerd has been assassinated!"

A ripple of horror went through me. I hated violence of any kind; I didn't care who the victim was. Alan told me that a man had walked up to Verwoerd in the Houses of Parliament in Cape Town, just walked straight up to him and plunged this knife deep into his body in front of the whole assembly.

"Nobody knows who the man was who did it," Alan said. "But they've got him in custody."

When Emily heard, she started dancing up and down the kitchen. She even took Alan's hands and wanted to dance with him.

"But Emily," Alan said, "the next prime minister will be even worse! Especially if it's that Vorster."

"Hau, Baas Alan! You mustn't say that."

When I next saw Alan, which was on the weekend, he seemed changed. I didn't know if it was because of the assassination or because of the fact that he and I were together again. But he seemed less weird, and he was washed and shaved.

"They say that Tsafendas was mad when he stabbed Verwoerd," he said. "He was a bit of a religious nut. He even asked to be reclassified as a colored person, because he was fed up with being white. He said he was told by voices to kill Verwoerd. Sounds like he was used as a tokoloshe, hey?"

Alan took me to his room and showed me his latest watercolor. It was of a girl with bare breasts and her arms wide apart looking like Jesus on the cross. And below her was this kneeling bloke whose hands were either praying or cupped around her breasts.

"What's it supposed to be?" I asked.

"I don't know exactly," Alan said. "I suppose it's two people joined together in a symbolic act."

"It's well painted," I said, not being able to pay it any other compliment.

It was well painted, and he had captured the features of

my face and the color of my hair. And what's more, he had got my breasts just right as well—nothing exaggerated.

"You can have it, if you like," he said.

"I can't take it, Alan. If Mom sees that, she will surely have me locked in a deposit box at the Standard Bank for the rest of my life."

Alan laughed—the first time I had seen him laugh since Bobby's arrest—but he was disappointed.

"I don't see what's wrong with it. I think it is truly beautiful." He did, as well. He held it up to admire and smiled at me. "It really reminds me of being with you," he said.

"Maybe you should study fine art," I said.

14

In October there was a thunderstorm. There were good rains all over the Transvaal. Thousands of Joburg gardeners were now optimistic that the first signs of green would show through. In some parts of the western Transvaal, the rain was torrential, driven by gale-force winds which brought down telephone wires. Even in the Belt of Sorrow there was now a promise of the first rainfall for many months.

Joyful church members were convinced that their prayers had brought the rain. "Our prayers definitely helped, of course."

But the rains didn't last, and the level in the Vaaldam didn't rise. Most of the water fell outside the catchment area, so the rain was simply absorbed by the desiccated soil.

And the government banned the Beatles from being played on the radio. You know why? Simply because John Lennon had stated that the Beatles were more popular than Jesus Christ.

15

A few weeks later I missed my period.

I got edgy as anything, and every day that the period didn't come I got more panicky. Eventually I had to tell Alan.

"Do you know what Mom will do if I'm pregnant?" I asked him.

"Hold your horses!" Alan said. "There's ways of having a pregnancy terminated. I'll ask Merv. He knows about these things. You shouldn't have led me on that night, Ruth."

"What?" I said. "It was you leading me on! I was just passive."

"No way!" Alan said. "You were a real tease. But I liked it and I like you."

I couldn't believe that he had perceived the evening so differently from me.

When Alan spoke to Merv, he suggested we go to this Dr. Marcus, who did abortions on the sly.

"I can't give him my real name," I said, as we entered Lister Building holding hands. "I'm going to say my name is Felicity Green, OK?"

Dr. Marcus was middle-aged, and you could see by his expression that he could be bribed to do something on the sly.

"Rightio, Miss Green. What's the problem?"

I explained that I thought I was pregnant, and that if I was, I couldn't possibly think of having a baby, and that an abortion was the only solution, and we had heard that he might possibly know of someone who might do an abortion for us.

"First, let's do a urine test, and then we'll examine you, Miss Green."

After the test I lay on his bed, and he spent the next five minutes giving me this thorough examination.

"OK, you can dress," he said, settling down behind his desk again and writing notes on my card. "It's highly improbable that you're pregnant," he said, "seeing as you have never been properly penetrated."

"What?" I asked.

"That's right, Miss Green. You are still intact. In other words, you are still a virgin, and it won't be necessary to find someone who will perform an abortion for you after all."

I couldn't believe it.

"But my period hasn't come. I'm always so regular."

"Well, your period is certainly late, but I can prescribe something for you that will bring it on within a day or two."

"Thank you," I said, greatly relieved.

"And by the next time you and your boyfriend wish to be intimate, may I suggest that you are on the Pill or that you use a prophylactic. You never know, next time he might find the way in, and unless you are using contraception, you might still have need of that backstreet abortion."

I've never been so embarrassed in all my life. No wonder Alan had given up all idea of becoming an obstetrician! He didn't have a clue! It struck me that Larry would have found the way in all right.

16

I never liked going to shul much. But Mom always insisted that I attend synagogue on both days of the Jewish New Year and on the Day of Atonement, because that's the holiest day of the year.

That only totaled three days a year, but still it was too much for me. I didn't want to go at all that year, but in the end I compromised and made it a one-day visit—just the Day of Atonement.

It was about the only time that Mannie, Mom, Lenore, and I were together in the Zephyr 6. I suppose that's what holy days do to people. We parked, as usual, quite a way from the shul because Mom didn't want it widely known that we had used the car on such a holy day. But of course, when she parked the car, all her friends and neighbors were parking their cars too, so she couldn't hide the fact from them after all.

Mom had her seat upstairs with all the other women, and I found a spare seat somewhere up at the top. From here you had a good view of all the men downstairs, and you could tell easily which of them were religious by how often their eyes strayed upward. I don't mean upward to heaven

—no, just upward to upstairs, where the women were. There were some eyes that looked upward throughout the service; upward and in wide circles, taking in every upstairs seat in the whole synagogue. And all the yiddishe mamas and their daughters were togged out in clothes and hats bought especially for such holy days. This year, the holy fashion was the mini, which had really caught on since the Durban July, in spite of being blamed for the drought. It was cool anyhow, what with the summer just beginning. And hairstyles ranged from superlarge beehive to ordinary beehive, with full fringes. Those men's eyes just feasted on the fashion show, even though their stomachs were fasting for twenty-four hours.

Mannie's seat was near the bimah where the rabbi mumbled through the service as speedily as humanly possible, interrupted only by heartrending songs.

Just below the bimah were seats for the three big shots of the synagogue. They sat there with their top hats, looking smugly superior, as though they had nothing much to atone for and were on good business terms with the Almighty. I didn't usually give those guys a second glance, until I recognized one of them.

It was Ullman!

How that man had the audacity to sit there like that, only he knew! Because I didn't. He must have had enormous cheek to sit there so calmly on the Day of Atonement without so much as hiding his head in shame. On the contrary, he looked damned pleased with himself.

I wanted to stand up and say something, or at least write a note to the rabbi to get that man out of the building. But I just sat silently and let the men's eyes wander over me until the service was finished.

Then the ram's horn was given a loud, final blast. What on earth did a ram's horn have to do with our modern lives? Not one person in that synagogue was a farmer, I bet. Talk about a prehistoric ritual!

Alan never went to shul. His family was not that way inclined either. Even though they were under great stress, they didn't show up, which confirmed Mom's view, after all, that they were non-Jewish.

"I can't see that one day is more special than another," Alan told me. "Nor is one building more special than another that I have to go there."

I had to admire Alan. He thought about everything so seriously and stuck to his beliefs.

17

The protests for Bobby and Ben to be released were gaining momentum, especially when Mr. Gerber established that Bobby's visit to Basutoland had been nothing more than to attend a conference on law and morality, sponsored by some voluntary organization. So much for that bit of subversive activity.

The National Union of South African Students appealed to the government to stop police harassment of students and called for Bobby's and Ben's immediate release. The government ignored the call and insisted that the students in the union were the true enemies of South Africa.

Mr. Gerber acquired the services of a well-known lawyer to organize some sort of campaign to put pressure on the government for Bobby's release, and the protest meetings grew in size.

I went along frequently even though my matric exams were just around the corner. I regularly saw quite a few of the people from Bobby's house in Parktown: Anna, the poetess; Patrick, the artist; and Greg, with the huge black beard.

But a person I didn't expect to see at these protests started coming regularly. It was Cyril. He stood next to us, and it didn't matter anymore to me what his sexual preferences were. He was standing up for Bobby and Ben, and that counted a lot in my book.

Mom couldn't handle me going to these protests. I was sure her worrying wasn't good for her blood pressure. But what could I do? I explained to her that it was the most urgent thing in my life. She couldn't understand.

"Oy, Ruthie, what good can come of this, tell me?"

I tried to tell her, but she crumpled into her wet heap, as usual, and another box of Pond's tissues got used up.

"You're very headstrong," Mannie said to me, as I was going to one of these meetings one day. "No good will come of it."

18

At the end of October, I agreed to go with Larry to one of the rave-ups at Alwyn's house.

It came as a terrible upset to Alan, but I didn't belong to anyone so I couldn't see what was wrong with it.

I told him I needed to find out how I felt about things.

I didn't mean I didn't like him, just that I wanted to sort myself out.

Alan wasn't happy, and to tell the truth, it didn't make all that much sense to me. But I knew I wanted to go out with Larry again; there was something in me that wanted to prove things to him.

By midnight Larry had me pushed up against this wall, and I could feel things stirring between us, especially just below his waist level. Obviously the old electricity was still sparking off at a high voltage.

After some hot kissing, we drifted off to Alwyn's bedroom, but we found it occupied, so we settled for another bedroom, though we didn't know whose it was.

The bed was soft, and Larry was very excited that I was finally yielding to him. I was excited too, but as his hand came toward my body, I looked up at his luminous green eyes and panicked. I just knew that he wouldn't like the real me.

Those eyes of his flashed at me.

"Come on, Ruth! You know you want it."

"I don't know what I want," I said.

"Stop playing games with me!"

"I'm not, honestly," I said.

"Is it Alan?"

"Yes," I lied, thinking it was a good way out.

"Dammit all!" he said. "You drive me mad."

19

The matric exams came, and I wasn't very well prepared for them because of my involvement with protest demonstrations and Alan and Larry.

In the middle of the Latin paper, while I was trying to translate this passage about Pyramus and his lover Thisbe talking to each other through a small gap in the wall, it suddenly occurred to me that I didn't know who to go with to the matric dance. They had both asked me.

But the issue was solved that night. Alan came over, all excited.

"Bobby's going to be released tomorrow," he said.

My heart leaped with joy.

"He's been in there eighty-seven days," Alan said.

Eighty-seven days in solitary confinement! What an ordeal that must have been. The same thought must have crossed Alan's mind, because he looked terribly sad suddenly.

"I wonder what he'll be like," he said.

"It will take him some time to adjust, won't it?" I said. "I'd like to see him, but maybe I'll wait a few days, until he's had time to be with your family. Is Ben also being released?"

Alan shook his head. "No."

The joy I'd felt on hearing about Bobby's release was replaced by a stinging pain. How much longer would Ben have to stay in prison? How much more suffering would he have to endure? If Bobby was going to be released, why not Ben?

Alan agreed it was so unjust, but he was also elated at the thought of Bobby's return and wanted to tell me about the welcome home that the Gerbers were planning.

But I never heard all the details because Alan interrupted himself to ask me a question.

"How would you like to come on holiday with me?"

"I can't. I'm busy with exams."

"No, I mean when your term is finished."

"Mom will never allow it," I said.

"But what if we go with Merv and Adele? They're going for ten days. They've asked us to come with. You could tell your Mom you're going with Adele, and I could tell my folks I'm going with Merv."

"It sounds fabulous," I said. "But one condition."

"What's that?"

"That Larry takes me to the matric dance."

20

The morning of Bobby's release I was so excited. He was due to be released at noon, and I could hardly concentrate on the history paper. Who cared about the scramble for Africa?

As I came out of the hall I thought of Bobby. He's being released right now, I thought.

Mr. and Mrs. Gerber and Alan had gone up to Pretoria to bring him home, so I didn't want to ring them till about three in the afternoon. That would give them at least some time to settle down and have something to eat.

But before I could ring, Alan rolled up in the Borgward.

He looked absolutely awful. Just one look and I could tell something had gone badly wrong with Bobby's release.

"What's happened, Alan? Didn't they release him?"

"They did," he said. "Can you come in the car?"

As we rode along Jan Smuts Avenue he told me that when they got to Pretoria Central, they found that Bobby had been released an hour earlier. But he had been released in a police vehicle, accompanied by several officers, and what's more, the vehicle had driven directly to Jan Smuts Airport. There Bobby had been put on a plane bound for England.

This officer at the prison had the cheek to say it was Bobby's own choice.

"They gave him a choice, all right," Alan said. "Continued indefinite detention or a little journey to England?"

Alan was so choked he could hardly speak, but he told me that Bobby had been put straight on the plane with a piece of paper that wasn't even a passport. It was an exit permit. All it said was that Robert Gerber could never return to South Africa.

I burst into tears when he told me that. Alan stopped the car, and we held on to each other. The world seemed so cruel: its crocodile teeth could snap down at any time with someone you love inside.

My tears fell on Alan's shirt, and he caressed the top of my head.

"My father raced to Jan Smuts but the plane had just taken off. We didn't even see Bobby. He left without a good-bye."

I couldn't stop crying.

"Still, at least he's free. He doesn't know a soul in England, but at least he's free."

"Yes, thank God for that," I said. "But what about Ben?"

That question came out so awkwardly, it sounded as if I wasn't pleased that Bobby was free. But sometimes in the middle of all the fuss about Bobby I felt like I was the only one remembering Ben.

"He is still inside," Alan said.

"Aren't they going to release him?"

"No. He wasn't given any choices like Bobby was."

"How long will they still keep him in?"

"Who knows?" Alan held my hand. "We're all flying to England tomorrow, so really I've come to say good-bye."

I felt this pang of anxiety.

"But you're coming back, aren't you?"

"Of course. I suppose so. I don't know."

21

The matric dance came, and Larry was as handsome as ever in his smart three-piece suit, but my mind kept jumping back to the time I had danced with Ben. I couldn't believe that same person was locked up in some dingy cell at that very moment. And when my mind wasn't thinking of Ben, it hovered somewhere in a distant land where a family was being reunited and where plans for the future were being made.

The band was the Gonks, and they played all the latest hits. I was just starting to relax and enjoy dancing, when I looked up into Larry's green eyes and wondered what he was thinking.

He surprised me by asking if I'd heard that Gerrit Viljoen had been captured by the police.

"Oh God!" I said.

"He's going to get life imprisonment, for sure," he said. "They must have extracted the information about his whereabouts from Robert Gerber, don't you think?"

"How can you say that?" I said.

"I'm not being horrible," he said. "But they did torture Robert, so he might have blabbed. And now with Gerrit Viljoen's capture coming so soon after Robert's release, it makes you think, doesn't it?"

Later, when he realized how much he'd upset me, he turned on the charm and whispered sweet things to me. The girls at the dance loved the Austin Healey, and they whispered about Larry's good looks and how lucky I was. But when the Gonks played "Yesterday," I never felt so confused in my life.

22

Mom couldn't believe that I had bodged my exams. She made me promise I'd never see Alan again, but I refused point-blank.

"Mom, I don't even care if he wasn't Jewish. I don't care if he never becomes a doctor. I don't care if his brother is a communist or not. I don't even care if *he*'s a communist. I like him a lot and maybe even more than that. There's nothing you can do about it. And I'm going on holiday with Adele and Merv and Alan to Durban for ten days in all. He needs a rest after all the trauma he has been through. He has to make big decisions about what he's going to do next year. Please, Mom, you must understand."

"There's no way you'll go on holiday with him, my girl!" Mom said.

"I'm not going with him the way you think. I'll be in one room with Adele, and Alan will share with Merv."

Mom nearly had a cadenza.

"What will everyone say? Aunt Bertha will think you're a trollop, as if they haven't got a poor enough opinion of you already."

"They've got a poor opinion of everyone," I answered.

23

It was snowing in England. Alan had never seen snow like that. Everything was white, even the branches of trees, he said.

A flat had been found in Clapham for Bobby which he could share with another South African who was a friend of a friend, or something like that. From the window of the flat you could see roofs and chimneys, rows and rows of them. Bobby spent a lot of time at the window, looking out and up at the sky.

He was well, but disoriented. He found it difficult to go to the corner shop for supplies; the first time on his own, he had turned back.

"It's difficult to be so free," he told Alan. "Especially with Ben still inside."

Mr. and Mrs. Gerber enrolled Bobby at London University, where at least he could fill his time completing the course that had been so suddenly interrupted.

"He'll be OK in England," Alan said to me. "Especially if Dawn flies out to be with him. But he'll have scars forever, I think."

The Gerbers stayed with Bobby for three weeks.

"The thing that bothers me the most," Alan said, "is that he's forgotten how to laugh."

24

The holiday flat in Durban belonged to Merv's uncle. It was spacious, with two bedrooms and a lounge and a balcony overlooking the Indian Ocean.

Of course, Alan and I slept in one room and Merv and Adele in the other, because Mom had no way of ever finding out. And we took the precautions that Dr. Marcus had advised, so that I would have no worries about becoming pregnant this time.

We spent the days roasting on North Beach and dowsing ourselves in the Indian Ocean. I couldn't help being aware of the fact that it was this ocean in which my real father had drowned.

Emily had asked me to bring her back a small bottle of seawater because of its medicinal properties. I planned to do it on the last day of our holiday, but I never got round to it as it happened.

Alan was very sensitive about being on an all-whites beach. The only non-Europeans allowed were the few nannies who sat rocking white babies in their prams and the Indian waiter who came by every few minutes. "Samoosas! Samijis! Samoosas! Samijis!" he called out.

When he brought us our samoosas or sandwiches, Alan always gave him a tip and exchanged conversation with him.

"Tank you, sir," the man would say, pocketing his tip.

"You like your job?" Alan asked one time.

"Very good job, sir, very good."

"But it would be better if the beach was mixed, all races, wouldn't it?" Alan asked.

"Oh, not at all, sir."

"Why not?"

"The tips from the nonwhites are no good, sir."

Later Alan shook his head over the Indian waiter's answer.

"It's all perspective, isn't it? It's where you stand when you look at a situation. That waiter can't think beyond his livelihood. Unless he's just saying that for us. . . ."

25

This young blond boy stood in a pit that was writhing with snakes. He couldn't have been more than eighteen years of age. He wore a khaki safari suit, and all he had with him was a stick with a mechanical tweezer at the end of it which he operated from the handle of the stick. With this gadget he picked up lethally poisonous snakes: mambas, puff adders, and boomslangs. That boy had no fear. He stood in the middle of about a hundred snakes. Some of them slithered around right near his feet, and some hung from a thorn tree right over his head. That guy must have loved living close to death. Then it was feeding time. He opened a cardboard box, and the food for those snakes scampered out. That's right, the food was alive! There were about twenty mice, and the poor things were stuck in that snake pit with nowhere to run. They tried, and some of them survived a few minutes, but as certain as anything, none of them survived for long. How could they? The only choice they had was death by puff adder or death by mamba or death by boomslang, and come to think of it, they didn't even have that choice. Right in front of us we watched one mouse paralyzed by fear even before it felt the fangs of a puff adder sink into its little body. The blond bloke explained to the audience of about twenty people how deadly those snakes were. "You'd be dead within minutes if one of those bit you."

Afterward, he brought out a large python called Valentino and asked if anyone from the audience wanted to have it draped around their shoulders. Of course, Alan the big-game hunter volunteered, and I took his photo.

26

Alan did a lot of thinking that holiday. Mostly his thoughts kept wandering across the ocean to England, or across the land to Pretoria where Ben was still trapped.

But he also decided he would do anthropology and philosophy the following year. I was surprised in a way. I thought he might go back to medicine and take the exams which he'd missed by going to England.

"Are you disappointed, Ruth?"

"Not really. I think you'll do well at something you enjoy."

"What are you going to do?" he asked me.

"I don't know," I said. "I must make up my mind. I only hope I didn't muck up my exams so badly that I don't get into university."

I had been doing a lot of thinking myself. Not only about Bobby and Ben, but also about how much I had changed politically. My God, I thought, how narrow I used to be in my attitudes!

I also thought a lot about Alan and me. We had been through so much together, and we even spent the hours on the beach discussing what could be done to help free Ben. I felt good about our relationship, and I came to the conclusion that I didn't need to prove anything with Larry anymore.

We had been in Durban six days when a message came through to the block of flats where we were staying. It said to phone home immediately.

I couldn't understand what Mom wanted from me so urgently, but when I phoned it wasn't Mom who answered—it was Mannie.

"Ruth, is it you? You must come home right away. We were burgled last night."

"Burgled? Did they take much?"

"Not so much, but come home right away."

"Why must I come home?"

"It's your mother, Ruth. She's very ill. I'm so worried about her. Please come home right away. She needs you."

"Why? For God's sake, what's wrong with her?"

"She's in hospital. She just collapsed this morning, and Dr. Glass called for the ambulance. Please come back right away. Get a plane. Oh God, I hope she pulls through."

"All right, I'll get there as soon as I can."

Alan was very understanding.

"I'll come with you," he said.

Merv was also great.

"If you can't get on the plane, we'll drive you back. It's only three days early. We don't mind, do we, Dellie?"

PART SEVEN

1

W HEN M OM PASSED AWAY, MY WHOLE WORLD passed away. It never would be the same again. I never knew how much I loved her till she was gone. Nor how much she'd done for me.

A gap was left on the earth that nobody could fill—ever. I was truly living in a Belt of Sorrow, and no rain could ever fall again to make things grow.

It was strange: the person I most wanted to talk to about my sorrow was Mom. I longed to be able to go into the breakfast room late at night, when everyone else was asleep, and have one of our old heart-to-hearts. "Mom," I would say, "why did you have to leave us?"

Lenore was inconsolable. She turned to me for comfort, and she and I wept together. We had only each other.

Mannie wept in his own bedroom, where Mom's clothes filled the wardrobe and her scents pervaded the air. He wept unashamedly, with great gasping sobs.

2

Mom was on a drip when we'd got to the hospital. And sleeping. I sat with her for a long while, thinking of all the things I'd like to say to her. Mom, I love you so much; please get better soon. I'll try not to be such a trial to you. But I love Alan, and I hope you'll come to approve of him too. And Mom, I've decided to go to Wits and do speech therapy. You always wanted me to go to university, so you'll be pleased.

But she didn't open her eyes.

The doctor explained to me that it was touch and go. There was little the surgeons could do to help her chances of survival.

I hung around the hospital like a lost soul the whole day, but it was worth it because at quarter past five the doctors called me in to see her again.

Her eyes were open, but so vacant. Almost as if nobody was at home.

"Ruth," she said.

"Mom, it's me," I said, holding her frail hand, the one that didn't have the drip connected to it.

But she didn't say anything else.

Come on, Mom, I thought. Please don't leave me now. I need you so much. I want to talk to you and make you smile again. Please, Mom, come on! Open your eyes again, and I'll tell you about my holiday. I haven't got anyone else, Mom, just you. I haven't had a real dad for so long, but you've done a good job. Honestly, you've looked after me so well.

I held Mom's hand until a nurse came in and said it would be better if I left.

Mannie came in behind her and asked me if she'd woken up. I told him that she'd said my name.

"Can I stay with her for a while?" he asked me and the nurse, with tears rolling out of both his eyes. I left the room and left him there sitting quietly with her.

It was the last time I saw her.

3

In the morning the hospital phoned to say she had passed away peacefully in the early hours of the morning.

Mannie cried and cried.

"She was such a good woman," he howled. "Such a good woman."

When I went into the kitchen, Emily held me round.

"I'm sorry, Rootie," she said, crying. "She is my mother also."

4

The burglary must have taken place while Mannie and Mom had been out at the Greenbaums for bridge, because it was when they returned that they discovered the house had been broken into.

The bedroom had been ransacked, Mannie told me. All the underwear from the dressing table was strewn over the floor. The blankets had been stripped off Mom's bed and some dirt thrown on it. Handbags and perfume bottles had been pulled out of the top shelf of Mom's wardrobe and just dropped in a pile.

"He knew exactly what he was looking for and where to find it," Mannie said.

"What?"

"Your mother's jewelry and all her gold Krugerrands."

"I didn't know Mom had Krugerrands."

"Yes, she kept them tucked away up at the top of the cupboard. And the wedding ring from her first husband. I always told her to put them in the bank."

Mom had been shocked by the intrusion, obviously, and by the loss of so many rands' worth of jewelry and coins, but I knew from Mannie's description that the thing that must have upset her most was the loss of my real dad's diamond ring.

Still, she managed to cope with the police later that night when they came to investigate.

Emily's husband, Isaac, told the police there were three burglars. He said he'd seen them running off and tried to chase them.

And one of them, he said, was John, the garden boy we'd fired a couple of months earlier.

Isaac and John had never been on good terms, so my mom wasn't sure whether to believe his story. She felt Isaac might be taking advantage of the situation to put the blame on John.

But Mannie was convinced.

"Of course I knew it was that bladdy John right away. He knew which night we go to play bridge at the Greenbaums, and he knew where to look for the jewelry and Krugerrands."

I asked Mannie how John could possibly have known that those things were hidden there.

"They know everything about us, those people. They've been through all our drawers a hundred times while we're away. You think they're idiots?"

While the police were examining the room, they took note of the dirt that had been sprinkled on Mom's bed. At first they thought it was mixed herbs and spices. But then they realized: it was *muti*.

The police cross-questioned Mom to discover if any black person held a grudge against her and would want to put a curse on her.

She couldn't think of anyone, but Mannie insisted it must have been John. Mom couldn't believe it. She maintained that she had always been good to John, even though she had to fire him in the end.

But the thing that finally convinced Mom and everybody else that it might well have been John was when one policeman discovered that mixed in the *muti*, among the crushed leaves, were hundreds of old toenails!

5

It was the morning after the burglary that Mom took ill. She collapsed in the toilet. Dr. Glass came, examined her, and insisted she go to the general hospital immediately.

According to Mannie, Mom had got hysterical about finding the *muti* on her bed and refused to sleep there ever again. Mannie tried to persuade her that the *muti* was harmless, but Mom was beyond reason, he said. It frightened her terribly.

They had had one almighty argument, lasting most of the night, and from what Lenore told me, it was the worst row ever. Mom wouldn't sleep in that bed, and what's more, she wanted to move out of the room permanently.

But in the early hours of the morning she suddenly came to the realization that the *muti* might not have been intended for her. She remembered that she had swapped the position of her bed and Mannie's bed. And John wouldn't have known of the swapping, because he had left by then. Mom therefore reckoned the *muti* had actually been intended for Mannie!

Mannie denied it strongly! But Mom said it made sense; because surely it was *his* toenails in the *muti*. Lenore told me that Mannie got quite frantic himself at the suggestion that John had intended to sprinkle the *muti* on his bed. He wouldn't accept the idea at all and became more and more vehement that Mom should ignore all this hocus-pocus and that she should just go to sleep as usual.

Mom was petrified of lying down in her bed. But Mannie helped her turn the mattress and remake the bed with fresh sheets and blankets. And he sprayed air freshener on and around the bed.

In the end Mom was so fatigued that she did lie down on her bed, but only for half an hour. She felt so uncomfortable and so ill by then that she couldn't fall asleep, and anyway it was already dawn and the sunlight was beginning to stream through the curtains.

She went to the kitchen to boil the kettle to make herself a coffee. And in the toilet she suddenly collapsed.

6

The way Mannie told me all this he took pains to emphasize that he thought the *muti* business was all nonsense. According to Mannie, Mom died because she got herself worked up into such a frenzy and because she was so exhausted. She was always getting herself into hysterical states, he said, and he had warned her many times that it wasn't good for her health.

But when Lenore and I discussed all this later, I was astonished by her understanding of Mannie: she felt that he had been so frightened out of his wits that he wanted Mom to be the scapegoat who absorbed the power of the *muti* intended for him.

"If only you'd been there that night, Ruth," Lenore said to me, "you'd have stood up to Mannie and made Mom a bed on the sofa."

I didn't know what really happened that night. Or whether the *muti* had real power to harm a person. But I knew one thing: if it hadn't been for me and my Vibr-o-sonic Breast Massager, John would never have got fired in the first place. And he wouldn't have wanted revenge. It was a terrible truth I would have to live with.

7

At the funeral Mannie went to pieces. So did Lenore and I—we hung on to each other as we wept.

But what pained Mannie so much was that Mom was buried in a grave next to my real father, which she had reserved for herself all those years ago. It was something Mannie couldn't bear.

For the week during prayers he was miserable and respectful, and he said Kaddish with a most mournful voice.

The future was uncertain. The only definite thing was that Mannie would have to move out. Mom had left her entire estate, including the house and all its contents, to Lenore and myself. So Mannie would have to go. There was no way I would allow him to live in the same house as Lenore and myself.

But then it slowly dawned on me that Lenore and I couldn't stay on in the house alone.

Uncle Barney and Aunt Helen invited us to come and live with them. They did it tactfully and with genuine feeling. Whereas, when Uncle Harry and Bertha P-chinsky invited us to come and stay with them, it was obvious they blamed me for Mom's death nearly as much as they blamed Mannie. Anyway, nothing could persuade us to go and live in Klerksdorp, for God's sake.

One other option I considered was going to live at Bobby's old place in Parktown. But it wouldn't be the same there without Bobby, plus the fact that I never really fitted in there. Anyway, my memory of that place was all tied up with Ben, who was still rotting in a Pretoria prison cell without any prospect of freedom.

Also, of course, I now had Lenore to think of. After all, she was my sister, and I needed to look after her.

She and I talked it over day after day. It helped to pass the time, and at least it forced us to think about the future and not dwell on the past. In the end we decided on Barney and Helen's place. As Uncle Barney's house was in Joburg, I could still do my course at Wits University. And I'd still be in the same town as Alan. Lenore would have to change schools, but at least we'd be together.

Once we'd made that decision, it soon became evident to Mannie that the house and furniture were actually going to be sold. He was upset.

"Where will I go? Why can't I rent the house?"

But Percy Zlotkin, who was handling the estate, wouldn't hear of it.

Mannie wandered around the house like a dog without an owner. Finally, he mustered his resolve and came up to me in private. He said that he wanted something of Mom's to have, and could he have the Zephyr 6? Of course he'd pay toward it.

I spoke to Percy Zlotkin, suggesting that Mannie's wish be honored. So he clinched the deal with Mannie, who got that car very cheaply, considering it was less than a year old. He got it even cheaper because he pointed out that it had a dent on one bumper.

All through the week of prayers the Gerbers were very kind to Lenore and myself. They truly treated us like their own daughters. And Alan was a pillar of strength. I honestly don't know how I'd have coped without him.

One night the Gerbers invited Lenore and myself to a

simple meal, just to get us out of the house. After supper, we discussed our plans for the future.

"It's strange," I said, "I ran away from that house so many times this year. Now I'd give anything to have Mom back there. I'd never run away again."

Lenore looked at me. I tried to see what she was thinking.

She held out her hand and put it on my arm, stroking it softly. Lenore was never one for talking when she was upset.

After dinner I asked Alan to play the Mahler symphony for Lenore and me. It was the sort of music that made you feel there was more to life, that it wasn't meaningless.

But Mrs. Gerber said, "Maybe you shouldn't. When you're in mourning, you shouldn't listen to music for a year."

I'd completely forgotten; I wasn't deliberately trying to flout the custom. It was just something I felt like doing because I was so sad, and because I thought Lenore might also experience the beauty of Mahler's music.

The next morning Emily called me into the kitchen to discuss something important. She was very agitated and had to tell me, she said, about the goings-on while we'd been out the night before.

"The master, he robbed the madam's things last night, Rootie. It's true, Rootie. He and Baas Ullman, they come in the dark and they take boxes to the car. Many boxes. They take the master's statues and the elephants. But they also steal all the madam's tablecloths and the silver knives and forks from the cupboard and the plates and the madam's tea set."

I couldn't believe how low that Mannie could go. And to

think that for a while I believed he was upset about Mom.

"Let him have it, Emily. I'm not going to have a fight about it."

"He's no good, that man."

"I agree with you, Emily."

"Your father, the madam's first husband, he was a good man, Rootie. He love your mother. And he never shout like this master."

8

The day I moved house, there was something going on at the Levines next door. Mrs. Levine was holding poor Hymie and shouting at Betty.

"How could you do that in my house?" she was saying.

"What's going on next door?" I asked Emily.

"The madam found out that Betty makes money from the bathroom."

"What do you mean?"

"When the madam takes Hymie to the doctor every Thursday, Betty lets the people use the madam's bathroom."

"What for?"

"To wash and to have a shower or a bath."

"And she charges them money?"

"Yes. It's fifty cents for a bath."

"I thought she was running a shebeen there."

"No, Rootie. How can you think such things? Betty is very nice."

That morning Emily left. She had wanted to come with

Lenore and me to Uncle Barney's place, and we would have liked that too. But Uncle Barney already had a servant, so the best he could do was to find Emily new employment with decent people.

"Good-bye, Emily," I said, giving her a hug. "You will be all right, hey? If there's anything you ever need, you can phone me."

"Thank you, Rootie. Good-bye."

I gave her a slip of paper with Uncle Barney's telephone number, and I watched her drive off with her new employers.

I waved to her from the front gate. The lawn looked threadbare and yellower than ever—the drought still had not broken.

Later that day we handed over the house keys to the estate agent, and Alan came to collect Lenore and me in the Isabella.

As we drove off I took one last look at the house. It looked so bare without the acacialata tree.

G L O S S A R Y

AG ◆ Oh! (*Afrikaans*)

AIKONA ◆ No way! (an emphatic negative) (*South African slang*)

ASSEGAAI ◆ spear

BIMAH ◆ raised platform in synagogue on which rabbi stands to read the service (*Hebrew*)

BIOSCOPE ◆ cinema

BLADDY, BLERRIE ◆ bloody (*South African slang*)

BOEREWORS ◆ thick sausages (*Afrikaans*)

BRAAIVLEIS (or BRAAI) ◆ barbecue (*Afrikaans*)

BUNDU ◆ remote uncultivated region (*Zulu*)

CHARF ◆ to playfully mess around (*South African slang*)

DAGGA ◆ marijuana

FAH-FEE ◆ gambling game of Chinese origin played largely by black people

FANAGALO ◆ jargon language (*combination of English, Zulu, and Afrikaans*)

GROB ◆ gruesome, ugly, grimy (*Yiddish slang*)

HUCK ◆ nag (*Yiddish*)

JA ◆ yes (*Afrikaans*)

JAWL ◆ to play or mess around (*South African slang*)

KADDISH ◆ prayer said at funerals (*Hebrew*)

KAFFIR ◆ derogatory word used by whites for nonwhite people

KAFFIRBEER ◆ name given to a beer drunk mainly by black people

KAFFIRBOETIE ◆ literally means "kaffir brother"; derogatory expression for a white person who sides with black people against white domination

KIDDUSH ◆ prayer said over bread or wine on holy days (*Hebrew*)

KOPPIES ◆ hills (*Afrikaans*)

KUGEL ◆ literally means "cake"; a word used to refer to a girl, similar to English "tart" (*Yiddish*)

KWELA ◆ a style of penny-whistle music and dance (*Xhosa*)

LI-LO ◆ an inflatable mattress used for swimming

MATRIC ◆ matriculation exam (required for university entrance)

MBE ◆ Member of the Order of the British Empire

MIELIE-PAP ◆ ground maize

MOENIE WORRY NIE! ◆ Don't worry! (*half Afrikaans, half English*)

MUTI ◆ mysterious medicinal power associated with things and persons (*Zulu*)

NAARTJIE ◆ tangerine

OY GEVALT! ◆ Oh calamity! (*Yiddish*)

OY VAY! ◆ Oh dear! (*Yiddish*)

PANGA ◆ knife with a long blade of the sort used for cutting cane (*Zulu*)

PASS-BOOK ◆ a book that the South African government required black people to carry at all times, containing documentary permission for them to be in any white area

PICCANIN ◆ an African child (*European slang*)

PONDOKKIE ◆ little hut or shack (*South African slang*)

PONG ◆ smell (*South African*)

POOFFY ◆ dirty (*South African*)

POTZ ◆ idiot (*Yiddish*)

PT ◆ Physical Training

RAND ◆ South African currency, 100 cents

SAKABONA ◆ greetings (*Zulu*)

SCHLUCK ◆ aggravation, shock (*Yiddish*)

SHEBEEN ◆ a place for drinking liquor

SHIKSA ◆ derogatory expression for a non-Jewish girl or a black female (*Yiddish*)

SHLOEP ◆ to try to gain favor with someone (*Yiddish*)

SHUL ◆ synagogue (*Yiddish*)

SIS ◆ Yuck! (*South African*)

SJAMBOK ◆ a whip of dried hide

SKYFIE ◆ segment of citrus fruit (*Afrikaans*)

SPOEK ◆ ghost

SPRUIT ◆ a watercourse, dry except during rains (*Afrikaans*)

SQUIZZ ◆ look (*South African slang*)

STOEP ◆ veranda

TAIGEL ◆ (plural is **TAIGLACH**); syrup-coated biscuit shaped like a doughnut (*Yiddish*)

TOKOLOSHE ◆ a malevolent dwarflike creature with supernatural powers (*Zulu*)

TSOTSI ◆ thug (*South African slang*)

ZONGALULU ◆ long millipede that coils up when alarmed (*corruption of Zulu* **SONGOLOLO**)